A HOOD WIFE

A THUG LOVE STORY

B. RICHEMOND

Cole Hart
SIGNATURE NOVELS

Mailing List

To stay up to date on new releases, plus get information on contests, sneak peeks, and more,

Go To The Website Below...

www.colehartsignature.com

TEXT TO JOIN

To stay up to date on new releases, plus get exclusive information on contests, sneak peeks, and more...

Text ColeHartSig to (855)231-5230

KENYA

- Diapers
- Milk
- Always Maxi Pads
- Dove soap

J checked off every item on my list that I had memorized in my head while I smiled as I walked out of the Walgreens Pharmacy store with bags in my hands. With the twenty dollar bill that I found within the cushion seats of our living room couch, I was able to get me and my two year old baby sister, Layla, some items from the store. It had been almost two days, and I couldn't allow her to sleep another night without having any diapers on.

I potty trained her during the day, but at bedtime was the struggle. Lately, I've been doing a good job by just wrapping her up in my old t-shirts and throwing an extra comforter on the bed so she could sleep on it. Then when I thought about it, the dirty laundry was just money I didn't have so that I could do the laundry with every day. When I saw that twenty slip out of my mom's friend pocket that day, my eyes lit up. I waited until he walked out of the door and didn't hesitate to grab it and hid it. As much as I hated taking something that wasn't mine, I had to that day. Layla needed it more than anyone in that house, and with my cycle being only days away, I had to think of myself too.

Walking up to our apartment building that sat on 56 Street, I cringed at the smell of the trash that was piled up on the sidewalk. The hood was the hood and I learned to embrace it, but at times, I just wanted to ask God *why us?* Why couldn't my sister and I be amongst the blessed and the spoiled? Why couldn't we have home-cooked meals every day, nice clothes, and a two-parent household like most of my classmates did? I used to kick myself all the time about how unfair life was to us, but after realizing that complaining about it wouldn't change my situation, I sucked it up and dealt with things the best way I knew how.

I was only seventeen years old and was holding down the household better than our own mother was. I was a student by day on most days and a fulltime hustler at night. Whether I was in school or not, I got things done. Everyone in the hood respected me and my grind because they were aware of my situation. Some were fighting their own demons too, so nobody cared to judge me. The older folks just wished me the best and told me to stay safe in those streets.

Yvette wasn't shit to me and would never be in my eyes. I didn't fake any vibes with her or looked at her as if she was some type of mother figure because she wasn't. All she was good for was for lying on her back and satisfying her needs. Everything else around her didn't matter, including her kids. The lack of love and attention that she didn't give us always motivated me to stay on top of things and to never give up.

I stopped in front of the building when I spotted the black

Nissan Sentra that was parked outside. I rolled my eyes and took a deep breath as I walked inside because I knew that I was walking into some bullshit. I had put Layla to sleep before I left, and I was just hoping that she wasn't up from her nap by now.

"Hey, baby, how you doing?" I looked up to see Ms. Marie standing on her balcony waving at me.

"I am fine. And you?" I smiled and raised my bags up to show her that my hands weren't free to return the same gesture.

"I'm okay, you know. I just finished cooking, and I'm happy that I caught you in time. Once you settle in come upstairs with your sister so you both can eat, okay?" she said.

"Ok, thank you! I'm coming." I winked at her.

Ms. Marie was the sweetest woman on the block, and if she could feed the whole country she would. She was well aware of our situation and did her best to be very neighborly to us. Thanks to her, I knew how to cook certain meals, and the more time I spent with her in her apartment, the more I learned from her. Especially on how to take care of my hygiene and how to carry myself like a young lady. Yvette knew about the bond that Ms. Marie and I created and she would find herself marching upstairs in rage some days demanding that we leave Ms. Marie's place. There were days I would obey her rules just to keep the peace and other days I would risk getting that ass whooping from her. Yvette wasn't teaching me half of the things that Ms. Marie was and that's why I would thug it out sometimes. I had to think about how the qualities and traits that I possessed was going to help me down the line and help me survive. Yvette didn't understand that because her definition of survival was beyond the things I would do.

I power walked down the hall and my heart started racing when I heard Layla crying through those thin walls. She was up from her nap and was probably scared out of her mind because I was nowhere in sight. Yvette was like a stranger to her, and she didn't know a thing about comforting her own child. It was such a shame, but I vowed to always be there for Layla so I didn't give a fuck about what Yvette wasn't doing for her.

The minute I opened the front door the smell of sex just invaded my nostrils. Layla's eyes widened at the sight of me, and she ran towards me as if she hadn't seen me in years. I picked her up and caressed her back to calm her down, which always worked on her. She was soaked in urine and had snot dripping down her nose, and I couldn't wait to get her cleaned up. Then I was going to take her upstairs so that she could stuff her face for the day. Ms. Marie was heaven-sent, and she was the first person on my list that I was going to repay once I made it out this hell hole.

"It's okay, baby. I'm here. I got you. I'm going to take you a bath and we're gonna go upstairs to Ms. Marie so that we could eat, okay?" I whispered in her ear.

Her cries instantly turned into sniffles once she heard me mention Ms. Marie because she knew how kind she was to us. She rested her head on my chest and in so many words, she said thank you. I hugged her tightly because that was all that she needed. We were all that we got, and I couldn't let this lifestyle destroy her. So far, I had $5,000 saved up and stashed in the house. I prayed daily so that I wouldn't have to touch it and thanks to my good money management, I didn't have too. Some days were more tempting than others, but I knew I had to stick to my goal regardless. It was Layla and I's emergency fund, and once I come up with a plan, we were moving out for good and not turning back.

I bent down and slowly reached for the Dove soap in the bag and walked towards the bathroom. I placed my hand on Layla's head so that she wouldn't have to keep another picture of what she just witnessed in her mind. Yvette had no morals and I didn't doubt that Layla didn't see something that she wasn't supposed too before I walked in.

The moaning between Yvette and Archie's dirty ass could be

heard coming out of the room so loudly. The closer I got to the bedroom door, the more I could smell the musty trail that Archie left floating around the apartment. Keeping up with his hygiene was not a priority, and I couldn't for the life of me understand how Yvette allowed that man in her bed damn near every day. For those dead presidents, she had no standards. Once money was involved she was down for whatever the lick was just to keep money in her pockets.

I was standing in clear view and could see Archie's sweaty ass stroking Yvette's back out. She had no shame and didn't give a fuck that her daughter was running around crying and witnessing the things she was doing. Yvette was like a child who needed supervision at all times, and it was frustrating as hell. I left the apartment for only twenty minutes and she already had Archie balls deep inside of her. Yvette must've called him the second I turned my back, and once he got that call, he came running like a dog in heat.

I shook my head because I was so disgusted but not surprised. I had seen and went through so many things and they were more than the adults I knew out there. It was all because of Yvette and what she allowed to happen. She didn't care that she was raising two young girls who might one day be a victim to her actions and that's why I took the initiative to protect Layla and I the best way that I could.

"Damn! You could at least close the damn door!" I reached for the door handle and slammed the door shut.

The noise startled Layla and she began crying again.

"Sorry, baby… it's okay. I'm sorry," I said to her.

I quickly walked in the bathroom and got her undressed. I wanted to get her cleaned, dressed, and upstairs to Ms. Marie because we hadn't eaten a thing since we woke up.

Once I started scrubbing her body with the wash rag and soap, I could see her beautiful tanned skin shining through. Layla was so adorable and I couldn't for the life of me understand why Yvette would neglect her the way that she does. I didn't care that she didn't want to be a mother to me because I was old enough to take care of myself. As for Layla, she didn't know a damn thing about life and it was so unfair how Yvette was doing her.

Admiring Layla's skin complexion, I couldn't help but wonder who her father was. Even though I didn't know a thing about him, my guess was that he was a Hispanic man and nothing else. Yvette's customers came in all shapes and colors and there was no doubt in my mind that Layla's father was Hispanic. I just hope that when Layla gets older that she finds out who he is because Yvette wasn't going to budge when it came to that.

As for me, my father died when I was around Layla's age. At least that's what Yvette told me. So I knew nothing about mine either. Aside from my dark skin, natural thick hair, and my deep-set eyes, the only thing that Layla and I had in common were our dimples.

I admired Layla's brown almond-shaped eyes that would just make anyone's bad day turn bright. I poured water on her curls and smiled at the sound of her giggling and playing in the water. All I wanted to do was keep a smile on her face forever, and if I had to die trying, that's exactly what I was going to do.

When I found out that Yvette was pregnant with Layla, I thought that she had made a mistake by bringing another child into this world who she couldn't care for. Then when Layla was born and became my full responsibility, she turned out to be a responsibility that I never regret having. I loved Layla so much, and I wanted to do everything in my power to protect her. I wanted to be everything to her that Yvette wasn't to us. So I learned about life real fast and end up juggling a lot for my age. I didn't mind stepping up to the plate though. I told myself that one day that Layla and I will see it through and we would actually sit back and laugh at this shit later.

I then heard the bedroom door open and knew that Yvette was finally done degrading herself by making her few dollars for the day. Even though I didn't approve of her actions, she was still beautiful to me. Also from what I heard, the old-g's on the block said that she used to be one of the smartest women in her class back in high school and she also did about one year in college. Life obviously got the best of her, but at the end of the day, I didn't want to hear it. Layla and I didn't ask to be here and by the way she is enjoying her life, she didn't seem too bothered or stressed about the way her life turned out anyway.

I pulled the shower curtain closed hiding Layla's body from that creep just in case he came barging in like he always did. He walked around the apartment as if he owned it at times and respected no one's privacy. Layla and I didn't have a choice anyway because we slept on a twin-sized bed in the living room that Yvette pushed against a wall for us. The one bedroom was only for her and her business partners like she would say and I knew exactly what she meant by it. With everything she had going on, I didn't mind and preferred to be with Layla anyway. There was no telling what she was doing in there with those niggas, and I didn't want us to have any parts in that mess.

I heard the door knob to the bathroom door turning and gritted my teeth as I thought of our cheap ass landlord. Because we were on Section 8 he didn't feel the need to fix a damn thing in the apartment, not even the locks on the room doors and that's what bothered me the most. Yvette always had traffic coming and going in our place and because of that, I always had to rush myself whenever I used the bathroom.

The door swung open and just the sight of Yvette and Archie standing together made me wanted to throw up in my mouth. She stood next to him like he was the king of her castle, and I looked at her with disgust in my eyes because she was nothing to me.

"The next time you slam that damn door, I'm gonna show

you what being grown is all about. You don't pay no damn bills around here! Who the fuck do you think you are?" Archie snapped.

Yvette now had her arms crossed and the look in her eyes only meant one thing: that she agreed to the bullshit he was saying.

I looked down at Layla who was now sitting in the tub splashing the water and exhaled deeply. As much as I wanted to curse that nigga out, I held it all in just because of Layla. Layla kept me calm all the time and I didn't want to get locked up for putting my hands on a mother fucker like him. Or anyone else for that matter. I always thought about how lonely she would be if I was gone and the things that she would go through in the hands of Yvette.

"Do you hear me talking to you little girl?" He asked.

"Yes, I here you." I smirked.

He slammed the bathroom door and I could hear him and Yvette giggling and talking in the living room. I turned on the faucet in the tub and with the palms of my hands, I splashed some of the water on my face to cool myself down.

I was so heated that I could feel my blood pressure going up by the second. Layla was my peace and she was the only reason why Archie wasn't lying in that living room floor in his own blood. Every time I saw his face, I would have nothing but evil thoughts about him. Then I would stop and think to myself and realize how he was such a piece of shit and not even worth the jail time.

I hated when he was around and when he wasn't, he would still allow other men to come in and trick Yvette out. Yvette didn't give a fuck because that lifestyle kept her stomach full, money in her pockets, and God knows what else she benefited from it too.

Once I heard the front door close, I reached for the towel and quickly wrapped Layla's body with it. I walked out of the bathroom just to bump into Yvette in the hallway, and she had attitude written all over her face. For a second we stared each other down and my stomach started growling. It was not only because I was hungry but because I could smell Archie's musty ass all over her body including her breath.

"You need to start respecting him because if it wasn't for him and the things I do around here, y'all ass would be in the streets somewhere. I don't see you in here paying any bills so you need to fix that damn attitude." Yvette snapped.

I shook my head because she was well aware of everything that I did especially the things that she couldn't do her damn self. I didn't need to remind her because my actions spoke volumes. She wanted attention and a reason to provoke me so I wasn't giving it to her. Yvette loved drama and if she wasn't arguing with everyone else, she would start some shit with me. I was too humble and quiet for that anyway so I just allowed her to run her mouth about whatever she feels because at the end of the day, she still didn't matter to me.

"Yeah whatever." I walked passed her and went into the living room to get Layla dressed.

"Don't *yeah whatever* me. If you don't like it here, you know where the fuck you can go. And take that damn daughter of yours with you too. I don't need y'all here taking up space and getting in the way of my business. I can't even make a decent amount for the day without her ass running around here crying and shit. After today you better make arrangements for her, and I mean it. Find her ass a baby sitter or something because I have money to make and don't have time to be rocking no crying ass baby to sleep!" She yelled behind me.

Yvette had to be doing more than just selling pussy because right now, she was acting like a person on drugs. I couldn't believe my ears but then again, nothing she did or say was a surprise to me anymore. Not only did I have to worry about school and a way to feed us now. I had to find a baby sitter for

Layla while I was in school and that was going to be hard because I didn't trust a soul except for Ms. Marie.

She worked during the day so I knew that she wasn't an option and daycare would just drain our savings account. I needed a plan.

I replayed what she just said and realized that she had lost her damn mind and I was officially done with her. Whatever she had going on, I hope she seeks help soon. Once I find out what my next move is going to be, I'll be on my way and taking Layla with me too. Since Yvette loved herself more than she loved her own blood I was going to show her what being without us feel like. Even though she was my biological mother, I just can't wait until she gets a dose of her own medicine.

Once I got Layla dressed and ready, I grabbed her diaper bag and we were now on our way to Ms. Marie's. Leaving Yvette standing there to gather her thoughts because deep down inside she had to know that she wasn't right within.

CARTER

"*Y*ou ain't shit and you never will be shit! You're just like your father and I don't know how I was cursed with a child like you." My momma yelled from the kitchen.

It was Saturday evening and my momma was on her weekly rants again. Last week I was a useless ass mother fucker, now this week I wasn't shit just like my father. I sat in the living room in front of the TV trying to finish watching the last fifteen minutes of the show *Martin*. As hard as I tried to tune her out, I just couldn't.

"Now get your ass up and clean my damn house up! You've been sitting on your ass all day and haven't touched a thing." She walked over to me and started hitting me with the broom and dustpan.

"Ahhh." I winced in pain.

"Get yo ass up now!" She yelled again and dropped the broom and dustpan at my feet.

I jumped up and quickly picked up the broom and dustpan from off the floor. I started to rub the left side of my head because it was still sore from last week when she hit me with her shoe. And it was all because of a cup that *she* left in the kitchen sink that I had to clean up after her.

I kept telling myself to be patient because I was only three days away from my eighteen birthday and then I could finally leave her hell hole for good. That's what our neighbor Mr. Clark advised me to do. He was not only our neighbor though but my mentor as well. He knew about the things that was going on in our household and if it wasn't for him keeping me grounded at times, I don't know where I would be.

After taking what he said into consideration, I went and did some research online and he was right. It was best that I waited until I was the legal age so that I could do what I wanted to do. If the law ran into me on the streets there was a possibility that I could be placed in a group home and I wasn't down for that at all. I needed to be free and not in a room full of dudes with different personalities. I was already dealing with the different moods from her at home so I told myself to chill.

Now before Mr. Clark started putting two and two together about what I had going on, I was going through it real bad. There were days when my momma wouldn't allow me to eat or shower at home, and I would spend the day hungry and dirty. I went from going to school on an empty stomach to missing class some days because I couldn't focus enough to be in there. Then when Mr. Clark stepped in, I felt like he was my guardian angel who came to save me somehow. We kept our friendship on the low because I didn't want my momma finding out that he was looking out for me. I knew that one day I would really need him as a part of my plan, and I didn't want to ruin my chances of making it when it was time.

The days I couldn't eat or shower at home though, I did it at Mr. Clark's house when she would leave for work. His son Brad would also let me wear some of his clothes when mine got dirty too. I was only 140 pounds and 5 feet tall. With Brad being at least twice my size, all his clothes were too big on me. So I would just switch out my jeans every other day and wear Brad's shirts instead. Then when my weight started to pick back up from Mr. Clark soul food cooking, he started to buy me my own clothes which fitted me better. Then he advised that I keep the clothes stored at his house to avoid any more problems at home and I agreed.

Mr. Clark wanted to talk some sense into my momma and the one day he attempted to do so after I told him not too, she cursed him out for even saying hello to her. Ever since then, he only concerned himself about me and he vowed to stay far away from her as possible.

"You missed a spot!" Giovanni dropped an empty soda can on the floor which, rolled to my feet.

Our momma saw it and turned away as she continued preparing dinner in the kitchen, which I doubt I was getting any of it later.

Giovanni was my little brother by one year but we had different fathers though. Even though we shared some similar features because of our momma, anyone could tell that we didn't have the same father and I hated that.

I was dark-skinned with brown eyes and I kept my hair in a fro. Far as Giovanni, he was a mixed pretty boy looking kid. His father was Italian and our mother was African American. His skin was lighter than mine, and his green eyes made all the girls at school fall for him without having any conversation with them. Because of how everyone admired him, our momma favored him even more and it showed. Giovanni was always dressed in the latest and newest gear, and his shoe game was sick. He got a haircut every week and never went without a meal. Momma loved Giovanni like he was the only child that she ever gave birth to, and she wasn't ashamed of showing it either.

Because Giovanni was getting off the record child support payments from his father, she had to show his father that she was taking care of him to keep the payments coming in. That's why she kept him dressed and had him on point at all times.

Even though things seemed great with them, Giovanni was a situation of a married man who owned a few franchise restaurants in Miami. Giovanni's father was *paid* and to keep momma's ass quiet, he kept the hush money coming in faithfully every month. Regardless of the money though, she was still angry. She was angry that my father left her for another woman and she hadn't heard or seen from him since. Then when Giovanni's father disappointed on her ass too, she became someone we didn't know anymore.

Our momma always wanted to be the number one lady in our father's lives but they chose the other women instead. Through all the bullshit though, Giovanni father was able to temporarily heal her with money. Then I was considered a burden and an extra bill that she had to deal with because *my father wasn't shit* like she would say.

"What the fuck? Pick that shit up!" I snapped.

"Naw, you pick that shit up! You heard what momma said. Clean her damn house up ! You've been sitting on your ass all day." Giovanni laughed again.

Momma had her back turned in the kitchen and acted like she didn't hear a word Giovanni said to me. Whenever he would start with me, it would just go on deaf ears. When it came to Giovanni, he got away with everything and that's why I couldn't stand her.

I exhaled deeply and closed my eyes trying to calm myself down. I started to replay in my mind all the positive things that Mr. Clark say to me on a regular. Then my heart rate started to slow down when I realized that beefing with my blood brother wasn't worth it. I had saw red a few minutes ago and was close to beating Giovanni into a bloody coma if I hadn't given myself a second to think. I snapped out of the evil thoughts that I was having because in reality Giovanni didn't know any better.

Momma was putting so many negative things in his head that he was lost in her world of lies. She was trying to turn him against me and he couldn't even see that. She blinded him with money, clothes, and shoes. She knew how to get to him and all he cared about was looking fly. I wasn't tripping though because I knew that later on in life that everything that she is doing will turn around to bite her in the ass real soon. I just wished that Giovanni could see through her conniving ass ways because that would save him from being a victim to her drama later.

He bumped me on his way out of the house and I looked him up and down. He was fresh as fuck and I couldn't help but envy him. He had on the new red and black Jordan's that momma bought him, a matching fit to match, and he completed the look by wearing a Miami Heat fitted hat from our favorite team. Even the cologne he wore smelled expensive too. Giovanni was heading out to chill with his friends like he did every Saturday night, while me, on the other hand, wasn't allowed to go anywhere except to school and to run errands at the store for her every day.

I had so much rage and anger building up inside of me that sometimes I was afraid of what I might do when I finally let it all out. For now, I just had to keep my head up high and focus on the positive things in life.

"Clean this damn house up! I don't know what you're standing there daydreaming about but this shit needs to be done." Momma came from behind and pushed me to the floor.

I was indeed daydreaming while my stomach was growling too. She was in the kitchen throwing down but I knew that once dinner was done, I wasn't getting not even a bone from that pot and just thinking about it hurts.

I stood up to my feet and started sweeping the floor to get it over with. I knew that once she went to sleep for the night, I was going to sneak over to Mr. Clark's house to finally eat and shower for the day. She had a refrigerator in her room that she uses to store the food that she cooks in so I couldn't sneak food out even if I wanted too. Whenever she was in a good mood, she would offer me a plate but I knew that tonight was not the night. I wasn't tripping though because I had a backup plan and all I had to do was be patient.

THREE DAYS LATER

I WAS OFFICIALLY EIGHTEEN YEARS OLD AND WAS FEELING BETTER than ever. I had been waiting for this day since forever and couldn't wait to see what was in store for me. I opened my eyes to the sounds of momma arguing and my mood instantly changed. I sat up straight in the bed wondering who she was debating with but I couldn't make out the voice of the other person.

Giovanni was her golden child so I knew that it wasn't him. Then I stood up and looked on the top of the bunk and Giovanni was still sound asleep. I walked over to the bedroom door and cracked it open just to see Sergio, Giovanni's father, standing in the living room hovering over momma.

"What happened to our agreement huh? You just feel like you could do what you want without thinking of the consequences huh?" I heard Sergio say.

"I don't know... I'm sorry... but I didn't do any of those things that you are accusing me of, I swear. You can look at my phone if you want. I don't even know how that happened, when, or what." Momma cried to him.

For the first time in my life I saw a sensitive side to her and for a second, it touched me too. She was crying and pleading her case to him like her life depended on it. That check she was getting from him had her tripping and I couldn't believe how she was acting over him.

"What's going on?" I heard Giovanni whispered behind me.

"I don't know but they're arguing about something. Just stay quiet," I said.

Giovanni instantly woke up from his sleep when he heard his father's voice booming through the house. Regardless of what was going on, Sergio had always been a cool ass dude in my eyes. He was laid back, hardworking, and successful. I liked his style and told myself that someday I would be like him.

I could see why momma always did her best to impress him because a man of his stature couldn't have Giovanni walking around the streets looking any kind of way representing him. Sometimes, Sergio would shoot me some money whenever he stopped by, but momma would just turn around and take it from me anyway so I never had the opportunity to enjoy the money. Regardless if I was his son or not, the fact that he stopped to acknowledge me made me respect him even more. My beef wasn't with him, and by the way he shook my hands, I knew he felt the same way too. He knew momma was fucked up, and he didn't like how she handled things with me but his hands were tied, and he had to focus on who meant the most to them, which was Giovanni.

"You know what! I don't have time for this. After today, don't call my phone. I have to figure some things out and until I do, I don't want to hear anything from you. That was childish of you to do and I hope you take some time to think about what you did. Damn! I really can't believe that you did that!" Sergio yelled.

He walked out of the house and slammed the door, causing both Giovanni and I to jump. Giovanni didn't hesitate running out of the room in tears to momma. I tried pulling him back but he pulled himself away from my hold. He was looking for answers, and I doubt momma was going to give it to him.

I stood in place because I didn't know what else to do. I never had an emotional moment with her and I wasn't going to start now. She hadn't hugged me since I was four years old and that was on my first day of school. Everything after that had just been emotionless with her, so I grew up without receiving any love from her. Years later, it still didn't matter to me.

"What happened, momma? Talk to me! What's going on? Why did daddy just leave like that, and what do he mean that he doesn't want you to call him anymore?" Giovanni flooded her with questions hoping to get an answer out of her.

She rested her head on his chest and kept crying. She shook her head as if she didn't want to talk about it but Giovanni was anxious. The more he caressed her, the louder her cries got. She was crying so loud that I was afraid that the neighbors might hear her and think that we were doing something to her.

The bedroom door was now wide open exposing me standing at the door. She looked up at me and then came charging towards me like I was the enemy. I took a few steps back because I didn't know what to expect from her and I could see the hate in her eyes.

"Get yo ass out! Get out! You're eighteen now and could take care of yourself for now on. I am not responsible for you anymore. Get out! I couldn't wait for this day to come and now that it's here. Leave!!" She pushed me.

Little did she know, I couldn't wait for this day also. I walked over to my closet and grabbed my emergency bag that I already had packed in there. I kept some hygiene products in it, one pair of shoes, two pairs of pants, and two t-shirts. I even had $1,000 saved up that Mr. Clark gave me from time to time for food. Instead of spending the money, I just ate his dinners from his house and saved the money because I knew I would need it like I do now. I knew the day would come when that witch would kick me out but I didn't think she would choose my damn birthday to do so.

Giovanni stood still with his mouth wide open as he watched me grab my things and walk passed him. I only had on an undershirt, basketball shorts on, with no shoes on my feet. She didn't even give me a chance to get fully dressed because she was that angry. I didn't care though because deep down inside I was happy that I was getting away from her toxic ass. If I didn't leave there was no telling how my day was going to be especially after Sergio walked out on her ass.

"And don't you ever come back! You hear me? Don't you ever let me catch you in here!" She yelled behind me.

I was now walking down the block smiling to myself because I felt so relieved. I saw a few of my classmates walking to school on my block whispering to themselves but I just ignored them. I stopped on the sidewalk and took the shoes out of my bag along with one of my t-shirts and put them on. Then I unzipped one of the pockets in front of my book-bag and pulled out the track phone that I kept in there also.

I texted Brad and Mr. Clark to let them know what was going on and that I would contact them as soon as I can.

It was my birthday and one of the saddest and happiest days of my life. Not only did I get kicked out but I left her house feeling satisfied and proud of myself.

A few days ago while I was chilling in Brad's room, he was laughing and chatting on Facebook with a few of his friends from school. When an idea popped up in my head, I asked Brad if I could use his profile and he let me. After a quick search, I was able to find Sergio's Facebook page along with his wife and it felt like Christmas Day to me.

I instant messaged her and to my surprise, she replied back instantly. After an hour conversation on the phone with her and sending pictures of Giovanni and proof that I wasn't lying about what I called her about, she was livid after our phone call and I knew that my plan was going to work.

So not only did Sergio's wife know about Giovanni now, she

also packed her shit and left him the same day. So that surprise visit that my momma got from Sergio, definitely surprised her. It was my gift to her because I didn't want to leave without leaving her with the same pain that I had to endure. Because of her greed and nasty ways, Sergio was now stopping all funds and didn't want any communication with her for now. She not only ruined things for Giovanni but for her too. Thanks to the patience I had, everything turned out perfectly in my favor and I was out her damn house. She thought I was going to be the only one losing, but she took a loss too. I was now on my way to starting a new life without her, and was going wherever the wind took me, which is far away from her.

Karma's a bitch!

KENYA

*I*t was finally Friday and I exhaled deeply as I thought about the school day finally being over. I hated school and everyone in that damn place. I wasn't dumb or anything, it was just an uncomfortable place to be in for so many hours. I didn't dress like everyone and didn't care about making friends either. Because of that I was the outcast, and I was okay with that. That was another reason why I couldn't stand Yvette because she made enough money selling pussy that I could've went to school in designers if she wanted me too.

Yvette was so selfish and the way my classmate's mother's cared for them, she could never compare.

As much as I thought about tapping into my savings on some days so that I could go on a shopping spree to show out, I rejected the idea each time. In my heart, I couldn't impress the people who didn't care about me nor save me and my sister if we were to ever have a damn emergency. My savings was for us and us only. So I spent my days in school walking the hallways saying *fuck you* to everyone in my head. As long as my grades were good, I didn't give a damn about anything else at school.

My frown turned into a smile when I thought about the

21

school lunch that I saved for Layla. It was pizza day and I saved it for her along with a chocolate chip cookie. Ms. Marie worked late on Fridays so I knew that I had to come up with some money for dinner tonight. In the meantime, I had some lunch in my book-bag that would hold Layla down until.

Then when I saw Archie's car parked outside, my mood instantly changed again. I just wanted to take a hot shower and at least take a nap before I had to go out there and hustle later tonight. Seeing his car just changed my plans because I couldn't stand when he was around. Now I was going to have to kill some time at the park with Layla until he leaves.

I ran up to the door because I knew that Layla was up at this time. And if Yvette was lying on her back again, most likely Layla would be up crying and walking around hungry as usual. When Yvette had company she didn't hear or see anything besides the dick that was going in and out of her.

When I opened the door, a rage of anger came over me. I scanned the living room with my eyes hoping to see Yvette around but she was nowhere in sight. Layla was sitting on Archie's lap watching TV and the sight of that just grossed me the fuck out.

Layla and I didn't know a damn thing about that man and I couldn't believe that Yvette left her to be alone with him. There were times when I contemplated on dropping out of school just so that I could be home with Layla. I knew how irresponsible Yvette could be and she just proved it today. Yvette always argued with me about how she was the mother and the adult in the house but I couldn't tell.

I dropped my book-bag on the floor and ran over to her. Layla kicked her feet with excitement and had her hands raised waiting for me to pick her up.

I gently removed her off of Archie's lap and hugged her tightly. Even though I was pissed off, I didn't want to show

22

Layla that I was. She was sensitive and I hated hearing her cry and she didn't like seeing me mad.

"Hello to you too!" Archie said with a scowl on his face.

"Where's Yvette? And why is Layla here with you by herself?" I rudely asked.

Archie didn't mean a thing to me and I wanted him to know that. He was sorry just like the rest of the men that Yvette brought up in here and it showed. The fact that he also brought men over for Yvette to make money for him definitely changed the way I viewed him and I had no respect for either one of them. She was just too blind to see that he was using her but on the other hand, she probably knew but her self-esteem was just too low to want better for herself.

"Your momma is at the store and you better watch who the fuck you're talking too. I'm old enough to be your damn daddy!" He stood up to his feet.

I rolled my eyes and walked over to pick up my book-bag because I simply didn't have time for him. He wasn't my daddy and could never be. Even my biological daddy didn't want to be my daddy so who the fuck was he? I didn't care what Yvette said about him being dead, I knew that he was out there somewhere. Just like Layla's father was.

Unlike some of the girls in the neighborhood, they were in need of a father's love but I wasn't. As long as I had Layla in my life and the skills and ability to hustle, nothing else mattered to me. Not even Yvette and she was my damn mother.

I was just focused on getting out her damn house because I promised Layla that I would. I didn't care if I had to put in overtime on the weekends when I hustled on the streets, I wanted us to be out of her place as soon as possible.

With my bag in one hand and Layla in the other, I started to walk towards the bathroom so that we could get ready to head out. I walked passed Archie avoiding to make any eye contact and from the distance between us, I could hear him breathing heavily and that wasn't a good sign.

I held Layla tightly and regretted that I didn't have my damn mace in my pocket. I always kept it near because it was the only thing that protected me on the streets. There was no telling who would run up on me one day and rob me or even worse, try to rape me. With all the mess Yvette had going on in her place, she wouldn't be able to protect me anyway so I kept my mace close. It's not like she cared enough about my safety anyway. I came and went whenever I pleased, but because of Layla, I never stayed out too long; only when she was asleep at night.

"Bring your ass over here!" Archie grabbed my arm and pushed me against the wall.

"Ahhh. Let me go!" I yelled.

Layla began to cry because her head had hit the wall too. I wanted to knock his ass out, but he had me pinned to the wall with no way of getting out. I held on to Layla as tight as I could because I was afraid of what he might do to her too.

The TV volume was up, and Ms. Marie wasn't home so I knew that we were fucked. My heart started racing. I didn't know what to do or what that fool had in mind.

"You think you grown, huh? You walk around here thinking you don't have to respect nobody, and you think you can get away with that? But I'm going to teach you today how to respect your elders." He laughed.

I could hear his belt unbuckling and his body was now pressed against mine. His pants quickly dropped to the floor and he used his other hand to unbutton mine. His breath smelled like shit and his body odor screamed that he hadn't showered in days. I was trying my best to hold my breath so I wouldn't have to smell him but I couldn't.

I tried to twist my body out of his hold but I couldn't and I was too afraid of letting Layla go. Her cry was making me panic and I was trying to reach for my book-bag with my right foot.

24

Hoping that I could pull my mace out of it and spray his nasty ass like the roach that he was.

"Oh don't fight it now. You a big girl ain't it? You gonna take this!"

He pulled Layla out of my hand and tossed her on the living room sofa. Something then came over me and I threw a punch at him. I hit his lip and blood instantly starting leaking from his mouth taking him by surprise.

"You fucking bitch!" He snapped.

He grabbed my neck and pinned me against the wall again. I was trying to fight him off of me but he was cutting off my airway with his hold and I was beginning to feel weak. I tried making eye contact with Layla but she was too hysterical to pay me any mind.

Layla wouldn't stop crying and tears began to roll down my face because I didn't know if she was hurt or not. She was too young to be going through this and it made the hate that I had for Yvette grow even more.

"Bitch I should kill you, better yet, put your pussy out there just like your damn momma. I could see it in your eyes. You ain't shit just like her and never will be. Like mother like daughter huh?" he said through clenched teeth.

"What the fuck is going on in here?" I heard Yvette say.

Between the sound of the TV and Layla crying, I didn't hear her come in, and neither did him.

Archie instantly released my hold and pushed me to the floor once he heard Yvette's voice.

"Oh my God, baby? What happened?" she said.

"He tried too..."

"I'm not talking to you! Why the fuck is he bleeding?" She yelled at me.

I was on the floor trying to catch my breath, and Layla was still on the sofa crying her life away. She walked passed her and ignored me even after witnessing her own nigga pushing me to the floor just to tend to him. That shit was so fucked up that it left me speechless.

"That girl is real disrespectful, Yvette! You better do something about her or I'm out. I ain't got time for no grown ass little girl to be disrespecting me and putting her hands on me. Look at my damn lip!" He protested and pointed at his lip.

I finally stood up to my feet because the look that she had in her eyes wasn't a good one. For once, I thought she would've convince me to love her again and trust her but as always, she failed us.

I shook my head and picked up my book-bag because the feeling of disappointment just came over me. Archie almost raped me and if she hadn't come in when she did, he would've took my damn virginity away just that quick. The sad part about it is that I don't think she would've gave a fuck if he did either.

"I should beat your damn ass! I leave this damn house for twenty minutes and I come back to this bullshit. If it wasn't for him you wouldn't even have a damn place to sleep or eat at. You should be thanking him, you ungrateful bitch! Not trying to fight him!" She yelled at me.

I ignored her insults and walked over to Layla to pick her up as I tried to calm her down. I thought about telling Yvette what her man was trying to do to me but she proved to me that there wasn't no point of doing that. It was obvious that Archie was her world, and Layla was mine. Just like she wasn't letting anyone get in the way of her and her man, I was doing the same about my little sister.

"When you decide what you want to do, Yvette, call me! I'm not going to spend another second in this damn place with that damn girl." Archie said.

He pulled up his pants and started to fasten his belt. I saw the look in Yvette's eyes but because she loved him the most, she ignored her gut feeling. The truth was staring her right in her face, and she knew what he was trying to do to me. But she was too scared to stand up to him so she looked the other way.

"Archie, don't leave... please... I can fix this," Yvette said.

"Do it now or I'm leaving for good! I ain't tolerating this disrespect, Yvette. I'm telling you now. It's either I go or she goes." Archie pointed at me.

I lowered my eyes to the floor because I couldn't believe my ears. I was only seventeen years old, still in high school, and I wasn't even old enough to rent my own place if I wanted too. *Where the fuck did they expect me to go?*

"I'm sorry, Kenya, but you have to leave. You're almost eighteen years old anyway, so I'm sure you will be fine. I can't deal with y'all fighting especially at a place where I make money at. You know I can't bring no attention to my place. You know that, Kenya! So you know what you have to do," she said.

Tears wouldn't stop flowing down my face as I thought about the decision that she just made. I walked passed her and Archie with Layla on my hip and rushed to the bathroom slamming the door behind me.

"Where the fuck do you think you are going? I hope you are going to pack and get your ass out of here!" He yelled behind me.

Once in the bathroom, I stood Layla to her feet and used my book bag to block the door next to her. I removed the lid from the top of the toilet and reached for the Mason jar that I kept hidden in the tank. I was able to hold the jar down with a rock that I kept inside of it and inside of it was where I stashed my money.

If she was kicking me out, I wasn't leaving her with a dime to splurge with if she found it. I knew that this day would come but I didn't think it would come like this. Not because of him. That was life though and I was damn sure ready for whatever came my way. I slowly placed the lid back on the toilet trying not to make any noise and I stuffed the Mason jar in my book bag and zipped it.

I turned on the faucet, wet my face, and quickly dried it. The last thing I wanted them to see was that I was stressing over the shit that they had just done to us. Little did they know, if I was leaving then so was Layla. There was no way in hell I was leaving Layla with her and that animal and I didn't give a fuck if she called the police or not.

I picked Layla up and stormed out of the bathroom. I reached for her shoes that was titled over by the sofa and quickly placed them on her feet. I didn't bother to pack any of our clothes or her diapers because I knew that I had enough money to get us anything we needed anyway.

"Where the fuck do you think you're going with her?" Yvette walked up to me and said.

"I'm not leaving her here with your pedophile ass boyfriend! And if you think about stopping me I have no problem calling the police and letting them know about everything that goes down in here too." I stood to my feet.

Beads of sweat started to form on her forehead because she knew about the lost that she couldn't afford to take.

Not only was she selling her pussy out the damn apartment, but she stored drugs and guns for the local dealers in the hood. Aside from the money that she was making in her bedroom, those niggas were cutting her a check too. Only difference was, Archie didn't know a thing about her extra income. She was pleading with her eyes for me not to mention it out loud and I stared at her with a wicked smile on my face.

"Let her ass go! She think she grown and could survive out there with a child. Let her ass find out the hard way. That little girl gonna turn out like her ass anyway. They will be just fine." He spat.

His words did nothing to me but motivate me, and all I did was smile to myself. Once I get back on my feet, I was going to make sure that I pay him a personal visit to show him how Layla and I survived without him and Yvette's toxic ass. The room fell silent, and to break the silence, I held on tightly to Layla and walked out the door.

I made it all the way out the gate and turned around to see if Yvette was in sight. I was willing to give her another chance, but she never appeared. Then when I didn't hear her crying and running behind us like any mother would, I knew that I made the best decision of my life just like she felt like she did with hers.

KENYA

*L*ayla and I had spent the rest of the evening chilling and hanging out at the park and it felt so good. Even though we were in a fucked up situation, I was happy that we got out of that place. After the shit that Archie pulled, there was no way I was going to be able to sleep comfortably in that place anyway. Also knowing that I spend half of the day in school anyway, I wouldn't be okay with Layla being in that house with them alone.

The ice cream truck had drove by and I had got us twenty dollar worth of stuff to hold us down until I make a move later. I also had gave Ms. Marie a call to fill her in on everything that had happened earlier and she just broke down in tears. I wanted to cry with her too but I couldn't. It was now me and Layla against the world, so I had to figure it all out for us, and I couldn't do it by worrying about Yvette's ass.

Instead of feeling sorry myself and sobbing on the phone with her, I just asked her if she was able to keep Layla for a few hours for me and she agreed.

I had a few bags of coke left that I had to get rid of once the sun goes down. The $5,000 that I had saved up was a decent amount for someone with no bills but now that Layla and I were on our own, I needed more.

A few hours later, I was walking out of Ms. Marie's apartment. Archie's car was gone but I knew that Yvette was inside doing God knows what. I placed my hoodie over my head, and with a few bags of coke stuffed in my bra, I made my way back over to the park.

The back of the park was my spot because that's where Teddy wanted me. He wanted the older heads to keep an eye on me who were trapping a few houses from where I stood. Then he always had a lookout riding on his bike, patrolling up and down the block. He was a good lookout and nothing went past him. He was suspicious of everyone who came on the block, even the mailman.

Even though what I was doing felt risky, I felt safe around those boys. They were like my extended family and each time I had to hug the block, I just prayed that we all made it back home safely. Teddy never understood why I chose to hustle because he knew that Yvette was getting paid especially by him. But because a resume and a legitimate reason wasn't required to sell drugs, he just put me to work and killed the extra sentimental stuff.

I didn't ask him any personal questions and once he peeped my vibe, he reframed from asking me any also.

After two hours of standing on the block, I had met my quota for the night and decided to wrap it up. I didn't want to stay out too late because I had to get to Layla. Ms. Marie had to go to work in the morning and I promised her that I would be back in time. Layla normally sleeps throughout the night but sometimes when she didn't feel my presence, she would wake up. I sent Ms. Marie a quick text letting her know that I would be on my way and headed to the corner store to get a gallon of milk for Layla.

As I started walking I could feel someone following behind

me. Sure enough I looked behind me and the lookout boy was riding his bike behind me. I placed my left hand in my sweater and wrapped my hand around my mace.

I had a long ass week and wasn't in the mood for anyone's bullshit especially him.

I kept looking back and he kept riding behind me as if he was doing some stalking type shit.

"You lost or something?" I stopped and said to him.

My heart started racing as he rode closer to me and when I finally seen his face, he wasn't no younger than me. We had to be around the same age, maybe one year apart.

"Naw I ain't lost. I was told to make sure that you make it home safe. That's all." He stopped his bike in front of me.

"By who?" I asked annoyed.

"By the boss man. Teddy!"

"Well tell him that I don't need no bodyguard. I'm good!" I spat.

"Why don't you call him and tell him yourself? I'm just doing what I'm paid to do and I ain't gonna let someone with a nasty attitude like you fuck that up for me," he said.

I twisted my neck and placed my right hand on my hip. He was the one following behind me without saying a word and apparently I am the problem.

"What attitude? I just don't need someone who I barely even know watching me. Like I said, tell Teddy I don't need your ass following behind me!" I snapped.

"I ain't got time for this! Suit yourself. And for future reference you gonna need more than that damn water-based mace if you gonna be out here hustling."

I stood in embarrassment because everyone knew that my mace was my baby. Since I've been working for Teddy, I only had to use it on three crack heads who were trying fight me for my product. Ever since then, everyone knew to come correct when buying from me. Some avoided me while others had no choice but to cop from me. I was left speechless and I watched as he rode his bike back to the direction of the park.

After I left the store, I finally got to the apartment building that I once resided in. I told myself to block out any ill-feelings that I had towards Yvette. I was only there for Layla and no one else.

Once Ms. Marie opened the door, that sad look in her eyes caused chills to run down my spine. I instantly knew that something was wrong, and it couldn't be about nobody other than Layla.

"I'm sorry, hunny, but she just took her and there was nothing I could do about it. I tried to stop her but she started swinging and I had to let her have that. I'm in no position to fight anyone," she cried.

"Who did what? What happened?" I placed the gallon of milk down by my feet.

Ms. Marie worked like a woman who was taking care of a village, and it showed physically. She was one step away from being handicap and the nerve of someone trying to challenge her. Everyone respected and loved Ms. Marie, and as I thought about what she said, it just hit me that the only person that would test her would be Yvette.

"Your mother... she took Layla. I had the balcony door open and Layla walked out once she heard Yvette's voice downstairs. Before I knew it, Yvette was banging on my door making threats, and she had Archie standing behind her backing her up. You know I am here by myself and I don't want no problems. I'm sorry baby... I just wish..."

"Don't cry, Ms. Marie; it's not your fault. You were just doing us a favor and I am thankful for that. I'll take care of it, trust me. I'll be back soon to check on you okay?" I leaned in and hugged her.

I didn't wait for a response from her, instead I ran downstairs and straight to Yvette's door. At this time, Layla should've been sleep, but I knew that her sleep was interfered because she was not in her comfort zone. Even though home didn't seem like home to me, it might've been to Layla. She didn't know any better and was too young to understand our situation. Those are the things I tried to make Yvette understand, but talking to her was like talking to a brick wall.

The sun was down and the hustlers was making money on the streets including Yvette. Her loyal customers normally came out around this time, so I knew that taking care of Layla would be the last thing on her mind.

I took a deep breath and started knocking on the door hoping that I was walking into no bullshit. I wasn't in the mood to fight or argue, but because it was about Layla, I was down for whatever at this point. All I really want is to take Layla with me, even though I didn't know where we were going next. I just wanted to be out of Yvette's hair but knowing her, she was going to make it hard for me because my independency intimidated her.

Ever since I was able to realize what was going on around me, I started taking care of myself. I never asked her for anything and only depended on her for shelter because I was underage. Other than that, I carried my own weight and moved how I wanted to.

The door swung open and a man who I didn't recognize was standing in front of me with a joint in his hand. The smell of ass, pussy, and weed exited the apartment and slapped me right in my face as usual. I was so disgusted that I wanted to just spit in his face, but I threw that idea out of my mind because I wasn't there for him.

"What you want little girl?" He asked rudely.

"Not you! Is Yvette in there?" I replied with an attitude.

His body was sloppy as hell and he didn't look any better than Archie. His two bottom teeth were missing, and his stomach was as big as a six month old pregnant woman. His breath could be smelled from where I was standing and the dirty weed he was smoking wasn't making it any better.

"Yo Yvette! There's a rude ass little girl at the door for you. You might wanna check her before I do and make me lose my high." He walked off, leaving me standing at the doorway.

When I didn't hear a response from Yvette, I slowly walked in and my eyes instantly landed on Layla who was sleeping on the bed. The sight of her brought a feeling of relief over me because when Ms. Marie mentioned that Yvette took her, I had so many negative thoughts running through my mind. I was happy that she was sleep but then again, there was no telling what type of evening she had with Yvette, especially with me not being around.

"What you making all that noise for? I told you I was coming out in a minute..." Yvette said and stopped once she saw me standing in her living room.

"You have company, and it's one with a bad ass attitude too." The unknown man said as he plopped himself on the couch.

"Listen... I'm just here for Layla and nothing else. You can go back to doing whatever you were doing once we leave. I don't want no problems." I walked over to Layla and began removing the blanket off of her.

"No the fuck you ain't! That's my damn child so you can walk right out that same door that you came in." She rushed over to me and pushed me to the floor.

"Ahhhhh damn!" I yelled.

"Get your ass up and out of here! I told you about bringing drama to my door. And why the fuck did you let her in?" She yelled and turn to the man and asked.

He shrugged his shoulders and kept his focus on his joint and I quickly stood up to my feet and went right over to Layla again. I attempted to pick her up and Yvette stepped in front of me blocking my way. I stood firmly in front of her because I couldn't believe that she was ready to go back and forth with me about my own sister. About a child who she doesn't even care for and hadn't shown love too since the day she was been born. Layla was more than a sister to me at this point, she was my child.

"Drama? All I'm trying to do is get her out of here before you ruin her like you almost did me. Look around, you ain't got time for her. And who is he? Customer number what?" I pointed at the man who was sitting on the couch obviously looking unbothered.

Yvette's bottom lip began to tremble and her eyes was turning red. She knew that I was telling the truth, and one thing she hated was seeing herself in the mirror. She looked over at the man and didn't even have anything to say because he was just that to her: another damn customer.

There was a brief silence between us but when her facial expression changed I didn't know what to expect until I felt her hand hit my face. I felt an instant stinging sensation on the left side of my face and because I still respected her in a way, I didn't hit her back.

"How dare you talk to me like that especially in front of... my... guest! You is one ungrateful ass bitch, you know? The things that I have done for you and your sister and you repay me by disrespecting me? So you think it's easy raising two girls without a damn man around, huh? You think I like doing the shit that I do? No, I don't! So before you judge and disrespect me, you better try to put yourself in my shoes. Until then, mind your damn business and get the fuck out my house!"

I stared her deep in her eyes to show her that her words meant nothing to me. I have classmates who are raised in single family homes and their mothers is making it happen the legal way and without a damn man. Their mothers may not be rich but they got the job done. Yvette thinks that her situation is special and that she is doing us a damn favor or something. Her sob story was going in one ear and out the other. There was no excuse for the life she chose to live and right now that's all I hear from her: excuses.

I could remember at the age of only six years old that I used to be in the stores helping her steal and lie all the time. And when her company used to come over I would have to sit in the living room with the TV volume blasting until they left. Every other day was a different kind of man in her room and not once did she ever show me a picture of my father. All I knew was that he was dead and nothing else.

I've witnessed her selling drugs, fighting with random women, and cursing people like her life depended on it. Crazy thing was she thought that those things were normal for a young girl like me at the time to witness. After what she showed me, I'll be damn if I let Layla go through the same thing I did. Luckily for me, I didn't allow those things to damage nor affect me though. I just want to save Layla before it's too late.

"Trust me, if I was in your shoes I would work my ass off and provide for my kids the *right* way. I wouldn't allow them to be exposed to this kind of lifestyle and if you think this is your only way out. Then you have a lot to learn Yvette! I'm only seventeen and I got this life thing figured out already, that's why I'm trying to keep Layla close. Look at him, do you think he cares about you?" I smirked.

We both looked over at the man and he was so zoned out that he didn't even realized that the attention was on him. His eyes was glued to the TV and he was still focused on his blunt. He didn't give a damn about what was going on around him including her. I could never understand how she couldn't see right through those fools because I did.

I then looked back at Yvette and I could see the look of embarrassment on her face. I wanted to feel sorry for her but I couldn't. She wasn't making her situation any better by allowing these men to degrade her and her own daughters were the least of her worries. Everything that Layla and I had was because of me. Yvette didn't give a fuck about what we ate or if we had any clothes on our backs to put on. As long as Archie kept money in her pockets and the boys on the block kept her on payroll, Layla and I didn't matter to her and it was a proven fact.

"You think it's easy huh? Well, guess what? It's not! Matter of fact, get your fucking sister and get the fuck out. I'm done talking! Don't you ever bring your ass up in here again, *Ms. Perfect!* Don't bring your ass up in her crying when those fools start doing you how they do me. Since you think you know it all, go and test the waters yourself."

I shook my head because her words didn't matter to me. Then when blood started dripping from her nose, my facial expression changed and she knew why. She was so embarrassed that she couldn't even look me in the eyes anymore and she quickly covered her nose.

"Trust me, I won't come back. But you take care of yourself now. You obviously have a lot going on too."

I looked down at Layla, and she was still sleeping so peacefully. I was just happy that she wasn't up to see the bullshit that was going on because nobody liked the sight of blood, not even me. I scooped Layla into my arms and placed her over my shoulder. I grabbed the blanket and covered her with it as I gently caressed her back.

I turned away and started walking out of the apartment feeling relieved while leaving Yvette standing in place with her hand still over her nose. We didn't deserve the things that she was putting us through, and I'd be damned if I let Layla stay another day with her too.

A few of our neighbors were now standing outside being nosy like their usual selves but I didn't care. I rather them witness me leaving Yvette's place than to know that we were still living with her and being mistreated.

"Damn that's fucked up!" I heard someone say.

By now, a few of them knew what was going on because

Yvette's voice could always be heard when she was going off on someone. The second my foot touched the sidewalk, I looked back and saw Yvette walking out with clothes in her hands.

"Get the fuck out and don't bring y'all asses in here no more! You hear me? Don't come back to my damn door!" She yelled.

She was obviously throwing out our clothes and anything that belonged to us. I couldn't believe my eyes and was so disappointed in her. She was not only selling her body but now selling her soul. She allowed drugs to interfere with her lifestyle, and by the looks of it, she wasn't coming back from it anytime soon.

I turned away and started to walk towards the main street ignoring every insult that was coming out of her mouth. With each step that I took, I started to see more of my neighbor's faces. I could hear some of them whispering to themselves while others yelled out for me to stay strong and keep my head up.

Whether they were spitting out good or bad things, I blocked out every last one of them. I started thinking about the new life that I was going to have with my sister and nothing else. I didn't know where I was going but I knew that I didn't want to go back to where we came from.

Suddenly my thoughts were interrupted when I felt someone following behind me. I was so spaced out that I didn't even realize that he had gotten so close to me. It was the lookout boy on his bike again and he was the last person that I wanted to see right now.

"So what you gonna do? Where are you going right now?" He asked.

"I don't know but I'm getting the fuck away from here. Maybe I'll go get me a room or something." I shrugged my shoulders.

The hood was so big but so small. News traveled fast, and I was for certain that he heard about us getting kicked out. If not, he wouldn't be following behind me asking me questions that didn't concern him.

"A room? You know that you're not old enough to get one right? Those people might just end up calling the police on you. Listen... just wait right here," he said.

"Hold up! How do you know how old I am anyway? And why are you still following me?" I stopped to ask.

"I told you already. Teddy wants to make sure that you are always okay. It's my job to make sure of that. And like I said, just wait. I just thought of something." I watched as he pulled out his phone to place a call and heard when he gave someone his location.

I stood in place like he asked, feeling confused and hungry too. My stomach was growling, I was feeling dirty, and at this point, I was tired and sleepy. Layla was also becoming too heavy for me to carry and I knew that it was only because I was feeling weak and tired.

We stared each other up and down for a few until a white Acura turned on the block and stopped in front of us. I looked at him and looked back at the car because I didn't know what the hell was going on.

"Get in. You have nothing to worry about," he said.

"Excuse me? For one, I don't even know your name. Why would I get in some stranger's car because you told me too?"

"Just calm down okay? Ain't nobody trying to kidnap y'all. We work for the same man so relax. But my name is Carter. If you don't want the police pulling up on you and DCF (Department of Children and Family) taking you and your sister away, you better get in if you're smart. You're only seventeen and your sister not even old enough to talk yet. I'm just trying to help you out, so what you wanna do? I can't force you so the choice is yours."

He got off his bike and opened the door to the back seat of the car for us. I stopped myself from saying something stupid and thought about what he was really saying. Even though I had money in my pockets, I was still stuck. I was underage and wouldn't even be able to get a room for the night even if I wanted to. The only person who would've been able to help us was Ms. Marie and that was out of the question right now. Even though I didn't know Teddy on a personal level, I never had to question his loyalty. One of his workers was here to help us and the reality of it was that I needed him. It was true what he said. If I walked away from this opportunity, there would be a high possibility that I could be separated from Layla before the sun comes up.

I always felt safe on the block and everyone who worked for Teddy respected me because it was only a hand full of girls working for him that was my age. So if Carter thought about trying us, I wouldn't hesitate to run my ass to Teddy to tell him about it.

"You know what...you're right... so where are we going?" I finally gave in and asked.

"To my place, I'm going to meet you there. You guys will be safe there and it has everything you guys will need so don't worry. Now hurry up and get in before the cops pull up. With all that noise Yvette is making back there she about to make the block hot and that's why I'm about to take my ass home too," he said.

I nodded my head and hopped in the backseat without saying another word. I had money and probably still some drugs in my bag. The police was the last person I wanted to see right now and with our current situation, I needed to be out of sight.

I greeted the female driver and kept a tight hold on Layla. Even though I didn't know her, I felt a little bit more comfortable that it wasn't a dude driving.

"How you doing? My name is Imani. I'm Carter's cousin." She looked back and smiled.

"I'm Kenya and this my little sister Layla." I smiled back.

Carter nodded his head and then closed the door. The second Imani pulled off I started to pray to God, asking him to keep us safe. I had no other options, and I had to trust that this situation was safe. Carter must've been our guardian angel or something, because at a time like this, we needed one, and he came right on time.

CARTER

*K*enya and her little sister were officially settled in my place and it felt weird and good at the same time having company around. They didn't cause any problems and they felt more like an asset than a liability to me. Kenya woke up early every day to make breakfast, she cleaned up behind herself, and didn't ask me for anything. She reminded me so much of myself and that's why I couldn't turn away from her situation that night. The first day I met her on the block, I saw a fire in her eyes like I never saw in girls her age before.

She wasn't running around the streets chasing boys, she didn't keep any friends, and she was all about her money. She made decent money too, and I never understood why she didn't spoil herself with the hair, clothes, and nails like most females did. Then when I got some background information on her, everything else became self- explanatory.

When Teddy called me and told me what was going on at Yvette's place, I rode my bike quickly over there. Then when I heard the messed up things that she was yelling out to Kenya, I decided to just stand by and wait it out. I didn't want to walk in on anything I wasn't supposed to, and by the things that Yvette was saying, it would make anyone feel embarrassed and hurt.

Teddy paid Yvette good money to keep his things stored at her place, and the last thing he needed was police showing up at her door because of her mouth. Yvette's place was convenient and easy to access whenever Teddy needed to pick up something. He made his own drop offs and pickups because he didn't trust anyone else doing it. Teddy needed Yvette for the time being and that's why he made sure that there wasn't any drama going down at her place because she was liable to just run her mouth if she was put under pressure by the police.

When I saw Kenya walking out with her sister in hand, I couldn't help but applaud her for leaving Yvette's toxic ass. Yvette reminded me so much of my momma and that's why I never cared for either. Just a week of living with Kenya she showed me that she was the total opposite from her momma. Kenya didn't allow Yvette to destroy and manipulate her and it made me respect her even more.

"So what's your plan? What you gonna do next?" I asked.

"What do you mean? You want me out of here or something?" She sat up straight on the sofa.

We were both sitting in the living room watching *BET* and Layla was sitting in her playpen playing with some toys that I had bought for her. I had been watching how Kenya moved all week and everything about her impressed me. She knew how to manage her money, pay bills, cook, and clean. Her mind was like no other and she was smart as hell too.

Kenya had it together like a woman twice her age and I could tell that with a little push, she could take over the world if she wanted too.

"Of course not.... We are family now. I'm just saying. It's been a week and you just been cooped up in here. I don't want you to feel like you're limiting yourself by being here. That's all."

"I'm not. I just been trying to get my head on right and think of my next move. Layla is not in school and I..."

"And you have me now. Listen.... I know it's a hard pill to swallow but you have to move on with your life and do what's best for you and Layla. I been there, done that. Sitting around thinking about how fucked up things are won't help. You just have to pick yourself back up and still make things happen. You already missed a whole week of school, and there's only two months left. Just focus on that and I'll do the rest."

Her facial expression said it all and my words had shocked me too. I couldn't believe that I was worrying about someone other than myself. In all honesty, I didn't want her going through the same things that I went through. Not only did she have herself to take care of, she had a little sister with her too and it made a man like me feel soft inside for her.

"I don't know what to say except for thank you. I really don't know where you came from but I appreciate you... we both do." She smiled at Layla.

"You're welcome. It's hard out here for us already, I just couldn't see you being out there alone. You are one of the hardest hustling females I know and it's to the point that you intimidate some of the older heads too. I like your style, your vibe, and the way you carry yourself. Just keep doing what you do," I said.

"Thank you but enough about me. What's your story?" She asked.

"What do you mean?"

"You know exactly what I mean. You aren't any older than me and you have your own everything. Your own place, car, and you have no kids. What's your deal?" She stared me deep in my eyes as she searched for answers.

"Honestly, I was damn near in the same situation like you not too long ago.. My momma wasn't shit and she treated me like it too. On my eighteen birthday she kicked me out but thanks to a family friend, I was able to get on my feet a little. Then being on my own required more money and that's when I got introduced to Teddy. Ever since then, I just been hustling and looking out for myself. Then when I pulled up on the block to check things out at Yvette's place, I couldn't help but intervene. Seeing you and your sister walk down that dark street didn't sit well with me especially knowing that I went through the same bullshit too." I explained.

We locked eyes for a few seconds and then tears started to escape her eyes. She was so beautiful but lonely inside. I could see that she was crying for help and needed someone to save her. She wanted someone to tell her that everything was going to be okay. I could only imagine how it's like living with Yvette. The drugs, the different men coming in and out of her apartment, and the non-stop verbal abuse.

Kenya and I were no different from each other and I wanted her to know that. I stood up from the sofa and went to sit next to her. I didn't say another word and I motioned for her to lay her head on my shoulder. I felt her body relax and I knew then that was all that she needed. Tears kept rolling down her face and within seconds, she started crying hysterically on my shoulder.

She had been carrying so much weight on her shoulders for so long that I could tell that she was tired. I felt her pain because I went through the same shit. Any mother who was willing to toss their kid out in the streets wasn't shit to me. Not only did Kenya have herself to care for but also her sister and I just don't understand how her mother could be so insensitive towards them.

Who would've ever thought that the little girl who was hustling on the block with me would share a similar story with me. She looked so innocent and quiet and I would've never guessed that she had all of that going on in her house. But one thing about survivors like us, we hide and carried our pain well.

I caressed her back because I knew that it wouldn't be long until things started to work out for her. I just needed her to have a little bit of faith.

"You can cry it all out today but tomorrow will be a brand new day and we will move forward from this. No more tears and no more feeling pity for ourselves. You got this far and I promise I won't let you go back. I'm here for you and your sister. Do you trust me?" I asked her.

She slowly lifted her head and I could see the calmness in her eyes. Her eyes alone answered my question and I knew from there that she was trusting me with her and her sisters life.

"Yes I do. You don't even know me and you have done so much for me and Layla. I don't know how I can repay you but one day I will. Thank you for everything. I never had nobody go all out for me like you did," she said.

Our eyes were locked in for a few seconds and spontaneously, I leaned in and kissed her. I was so nervous because it was technically my first time kissing a girl and I wasn't sure if I was doing it right.

When she didn't pull back or jump up, I guess it was a sign that everything was going good. Her tears felt so warm on my face and with a pretty face like hers, I was going to make sure that she never shed another tear ever again.

"Is it your first time?" She sat up and asked.

"Umm... yes.. is it yours?" I asked.

"Yes... I never kissed or did... you know..." She smiled.

My dick jumped at the thought of her mentioning that she was pure. I was too despite what other people thought. All the hustla's on the block would brag about the multiple girls they had sex with while me on the other hand, I just used to remain silent or ride my bike down the block when the conversations got heated.

Ever since I left home all I did was hustle. Adding a girl or girlfriend to my agenda was never a part of my plan. I was trying to survive and stack enough money so I wouldn't have to go down that road again. Then when I started working full and overtime for Teddy, school and girls were definitely out of my mind.

Even though I had my high school diploma, I didn't care about doing anything else. I always feared that the law would come looking for me if my name appeared in their system and send me back to my mother's someway, somehow. I was doing good for myself and didn't want a thing to do with her.

"Well that sounds good because I never did it either." I replied.

Before I could say anything else, she was undressing herself. I looked over at Layla's playpen and she had quickly dosed off in it. I didn't want my first time to be with a toddler staring down at my dick. The same respect I had for them, I had for myself too.

I followed suit, and within seconds, we were both naked. She reached for my head and escorted me inside the bedroom. I knew that after today that everything was going to be different between us, and I couldn't wait to experience more with her.

"How are they doing? Is everything good over there with them? Layla hadn't been crying or anything right?" Teddy asked.

"It's been going pretty good, and Layla is fine. She just eats and play all day. After having a long talk with Kenya, she actually went back to school today. She was able to get on some makeup work from her teacher and said she had a lot to do once she gets home. And everything is looking good for graduation for her. Her GPA wasn't affected so she's still on the right track." I explained.

"Okay good! That's what I like to hear. Whatever y'all need, just let me know. I know you gonna be good but I don't want them going back to that damn house again. Not only that but I definitely don't need them in the streets because Kenya is a smart girl and she don't belong there. Neither do you. That's why I'm happy that you guys are comfortable here and making this living arrangement work. If anything happen to you guys, that shit won't sit well with me so do what y'all have to do to survive." Teddy expressed deeply.

I could tell he was sensitive about the situation with them, well we all were. I wasn't too worried about me because I had been holding it down on my own but I understood where he was coming from. Imani was even doing her part by stopping by to take Kenya to the grocery store and also to the mall to get things for Kenya and Layla. We were all doing our best about this situation and to see Teddy step up like that. Meant a lot. He forgot that she was a worker and was treating her like a daughter that he never had and that said a lot about his character to me.

"Don't worry boss man. While she's here with me, she will have nothing to worry about. I'll protect her and her sister with my life. So whatever you need done for them, I got them too," I said with my chest out.

Even though I was young, I was responsible. I was loyal by nature and treated people how I wanted to be treated. This thing that Kenya was going through was nothing to me. Whether it was her or someone else, I would've helped anyone out who was in the same situation as her because that was the kind of person that I was.

"I appreciate it. That says a lot about you. But in the meantime, I need to go have a talk with their mother. There's some things I have to take care of with her."

"Things like what? I hope you not going over there to..."

"Oh naw nothing like that. Those girls have enough to deal with. I'm not gonna touch that lady and put that on me. Yvette will see the light one day, her karma is coming so I'm not going to waste my time with that. Anyway, those girls are underage remember so I need Yvette to give me guardianship over them. I don't want any legal problems with the law. If anything happens, I want to be prepared."

"I understand but what if she says no? What happens with them? " My heart was racing at the thought of losing them.

"I'm not worried about that. She has no choice but to cooperate because this is not a yes or no situation. It's either she does it or she dies and with the money that's coming through that place, I think she gonna want to go with option number one." He smirked.

"Yeah if she's smart she better get with the program. But damn, I never really thought about that. You know, getting paperwork on them and all."

"It's a must. In life you have to always make sure that you protect whatever it is that is valuable to you. The legal way is always the best way. You have to make sure that things are always written on paper and notarized too. Words don't mean a damn thing when those crackers come looking for you. Protect your homes, business, and money the legal way. Trust me. I've been doing this for years and I know. If you hang around me a little longer you will learn all that you need to know about how to really secure that bag."

"Don't worry boss man. I'm taking notes as we speak," I said.

"That's what I'm talking about but y'all take care. Call me if you need anything."

Teddy stood up and we dapped each other up. I knew that he had to leave and I didn't want to hold him up. Kenya and Layla had been happy here. Sleeping and eating very good and I didn't want anyone interrupting that for them. I couldn't imagine those folks coming in to pick them up so I was happy that Teddy was ten steps ahead of them. Now that Kenya and I was getting closer, I didn't want her going anywhere because I was here to protect her.

Teddy walked out of the house leaving me with so many heavy things to think about. All I ever did was hustled and put my money up but my mind never went beyond doing anything legal with it. Now that he gave me some insights, I had some things to brain storm about later.

Teddy was the man and I was going to do exactly what he said. If I hung around him long enough like he said, I know that I would learn everything about life and would be the man like him one day too.

KENYA

TEN YEARS LATER

"We got my main man Carter in the building. Ayyeee, happy birthday, my boy!" DJ Freeze voice boomed through the speakers as he lifted his cup in the air to greet Carter.

Carter and I hugged each other as we stood in the VIP section of Club Mansion in Miami Beach, enjoying each other presence. It was his birthday weekend and after working so hard this year, he wanted to turn up in the club just like we used to do before the *real* money started flowing in. We went from hustling on the block together and flipping anything that we could get our hands on, to not only being one of the best realtors in Miami, but the most talked about married couple there is out there. *Money House Realty Group* was rated number one in the city last year, and with hard work and dedication, we were trying to win that crown again this year.

Some people from our hood couldn't believe how two hustlers that came from nothing now owned and sold several properties in Miami. Even though we moved out the hood, we would still poke our heads in from time to time to show the people we used to fuck with some love. We didn't want anyone hating or thinking we forgot about them so we kept it loyal to the ones who kept the same energy with us back then.

50 cent's *I Get Money* song started blasting throughout the club and I stood back to watch Carter dance to his favorite song. We came from sharing a bottle of Ritz orange soda together to having our own bottle of liquor to drink from. Life was good, and I couldn't thank no one other than God for helping us make it through the struggle.

"Look at that boy! He about to fall on his face real soon if he don't sit his tipsy ass down somewhere." Imani walked up behind me and said in my ear.

Since the first day that Carter introduced me to his cousin, Imani and I had been inseparable. She was one of the realist people in my circle aside from Carter and no one was fucking with us. Whenever they saw me, they saw her. There was nothing that we wouldn't do for one another and we broke bread together because we were all family. While Carter and I managed the real estate end to our company in the office, Imani was on the other side providing credit counseling services. We were successful and our clients loved us because we provided quality and professional work. The fact that our business was family-owned was also a plus in the public's eye as well and we wanted to keep it that way. There were no outsiders involved, and we made a vow to keep it that way because the less hands that we had in the pot, the better.

"Leave my man alone. He trying to enjoy himself because he knows that after tonight, we gonna be stuck in that damn office until this tax season is over with." I yelled to her over the sound of the music playing.

"Yeah, you're right! I might as well join him too because I have clients calling me already too and it's that money season." She danced.

Imani grabbed the bottle of Patron off the table and took a few gulps. She then passed me the bottle and I did the same. We worked our asses off and on some days we wouldn't even go home because we were so swamped with work. We earned that number one title and that's because we all had a vision and goals to accomplish. Carter then walked over to me and pulled me in close. I knew he was horny as fuck at this point because I could feel his dick poking me through his pants. He stuck his tongue deep down inside my mouth and I slowly sucked on it trying to remove every drop of liquor that was sitting on his tongue.

"Damn that's what you want to do to me later huh?" He asked.

"The second we walk through the door. You know what's up." I smiled.

For the next hour, we danced to every damn song that the DJ spun around and we were all having fun. Then not soon after, Imani was stretched out on the leather sofa and I knew that she had checked out for the rest of the night. She was lightweight and it made Carter and I laugh each and every time because she thought she could hang and compete with us when it came to drinking. Luckily for us, we had a driver for the night. We were prepared so we wouldn't have to deal with dragging her ass out the club like we did before.

"What's good? Happy birthday boy!"

A few of Carter's associates walked into our VIP section and started dapping him up and wishing him a happy birthday. Carter had just wanted the night to be with us but he knew that once someone spotted him in the club, the whole hood was down to come out to turn up with him. He had street cred- itability and the fact that he chose to go legal with the dirty money he made, it made his homeboys respect him even more. Carter tried convincing them to do the same but their minds were still set on the fast life and he was okay with that. He learned to accept their decision like they did his but at the end they were all still cool.

"Aye baby. I'm gonna go to the restroom. This Patron is

running right through me. I can't stand around another second," I said to him, staring at him with low eyes.

"Hold up! I'm going to come with you because Imani's ass already done for the night. I should've been paying attention. Patron is not even your drink." He shook his head.

"Trust me, I said the same thing to myself. But tonight is your night and I want you to have some fun. Your homies came out to turn up with you. I have my phone with me and I won't be long." I held my phone up to his face.

"Are you sure? Cause those fools could wait!"

"Yes, I'm sure. I'm a big girl. I'll be right back."

I walked off leaving him with his company because it was his birthday weekend and I needed him to have some fun. He worked harder than Imani and I put together because he always wanted things to be on point. It made me smile to see him enjoying himself and not worrying about work like he always did. I had a birthday trip planned out for him too and he didn't even know it yet.

He had made a promise to me when we were younger that we would never be broke again and each day that he wakes up, he goes hard to prove that to me. I tried to think of ways to pay him back for the things he had done for me and Layla back then but I couldn't put a price on it. Carter was all man and he had been putting in work since day one without a doubt. I was blessed beyond measures and it was all because of him and the hard work we put together to make things possible.

I finally made it down the hall to the restroom and the club was so packed that I almost missed the entryway to it. Aside from the club being jammed packed, I was tipsy as hell and I didn't feel it until I started taking baby steps and it was now starting to hit me.

I pushed the door open and the smell of perfume, urine, and hair spray instantly upset my stomach. I ran to the closes stall and within seconds, I was bent over throwing up everything that was stored in my stomach from earlier that day. I felt like I was about to pass out each time the vomit left my mouth. I could also hear a woman leaving the stall next to me laughing as if she couldn't be the one in my shoes.

Patron was the devil and I tried my best to avoid drinking that damn drink. Thanks to Imani, here I was dealing with the outcome of it.

My stomach was now free of liquor and I reached for the toilet paper and wiped the residue that circled around my mouth. Without looking down at the vomit that was sitting in the toilet, I turned my head and stood up. Pressing my foot down on the handle and flushing it then I exited the stall. I was now regretting that I didn't allow Carter to escort me to the restroom because I was feeling sick as hell. And Imani was fucked up just like I was, even worst, so she was useless at this point.

"Can you meet me at the restroom baby? I'm ready to go home. I don't feel too good." I sent Carter a quick text message also feeling bad that I had to cut his night short.

I walked over to the sink, rinsed my mouth, and took baby steps walking out. The same odor that I picked up when walking in the restroom was now floating in the air of the club. I could feel myself getting close to throwing up again and with all the lights flashing, I was getting dizzy.

I started to lean on the wall and I closed my eyes hoping the dizzy feeling would go away soon. Finally, I felt Carter's touch and once in his arm I just placed my head on his chest and he guided the way. I kept my eyes closed in hopes that the dizziness would stop but it was getting worse with each step that I took. The more people that bumped into us, the nauseous I became.

I wrapped my arm around his waist and couldn't wait until we were out the club. He pushed the door open, but I finally opened my eyes when I realized that the walk seemed short, and

I could hear the noise from the club closing out and I didn't feel the outside air hit my face.

"Oh my God!!" I pulled away, almost slipping and falling on the wet floor.

"Don't worry. I got you, baby!" A man who I didn't recognize said.

I thought I was being escorted out the club by my husband and the whole time I had my arm wrapped around a damn stranger. My heart started to race as he began approaching me. All I had was my phone and I wanted to kick myself for it. I had no gun on me, no mace, not a damn thing. For as long as I could remember I stayed strapped especially with my mace and that's why I hated going to the clubs sometimes. People weren't allowed to bring in any weapons and even though I felt safe when Carter's around, I hated the feeling of not having something with me to protect me regardless of him.

"I don't know who you are but you better get the fuck out the way or..."

"Or what bitch! What the fuck you gonna do? You could barely stand up on your two feet out there. You lucky I came to save your ass!" He yelled at me as if I owed him something.

I could see the fury in his eyes and when I realized that we were all alone in the restroom and my head started spinning. I was too tipsy to try to put up a fight so I made a run for the door but he was faster than I was.

"Ughhhh!" I moaned out loud.

He grabbed my arms and pushed me against the wall causing a sharp pain in the middle of my back and my phone to fall on the floor. My heart ached for my phone too because I knew that the screen was fucked just like me. There was no way I was going to be able to call anyone for help now and for the first time, I was scared.

"You better thank me for helping you out there. Ain't too

many good men like me walking around nowadays." He licked his lips as he had me pinned to the wall.

I stared him deep in his eyes because I wanted him to remember me. I took a picture of every detail on his face down to the shoes that he wore. He was fucking with the wrong one and he didn't even know it. All he saw was a cute face, slim waist, and a fat ass when all I saw was death when I looked at him.

He was no taller than I was in height, his shiny beard was at least four inches long, and he had a lazy left eye that instantly caught my attention. Either he was tipsy or it was just a feature that he was born with. Whatever it was, I painted a perfect picture of him and he was dead to me.

He tried sticking his tongue inside my mouth and I tried my best to get out of his hold. This was the one time that I wished that I wasn't fucked up because whether he was a man or not, he would've felt these hands. I kept moving my face from side to side and with the little strength that I had in me, I was trying to fight my way out. The rejection was upsetting him and he began squeezing my hands. I felt like I was going to pass out in a matter of seconds because he was cutting off my circulation.

Tears started to form in my eyes. I didn't know what was going to happen next. I was tipsy as fuck, my phone was broken, and his ass obviously wanted to rape me.

"Bitches like you walk around the club with barely anything on and expect men like me to just stare and not be provoked. I tried being nice by helping you out and all you want to do is fight me off. All you women are the same, I swear."

"Get the fuck off of me! Do you even know who you are fucking with?" I yelled.

I looked at his eyes and it was as if he blacked out. Nothing I said registered to him, and before I could say anything else, Carter came running through the door with his boys behind him.

My eyes widened at the sight of him, and with every emotion in me, I began to cry. The lazy-eyed stranger then turned around, and once he saw the look in Carter's eyes, it was then that he knew that he had fucked up.

"My bad, man! I didn't know…. I swear…" The stranger pleaded.

I ran towards Carter and gave him a tight hug, thanking him for saving me.

"Hold on, baby," he said as he pulled away.

With a blink of an eye, the lazy eye dude was getting punch and stumped on by the crew including Carter. He cried and yelled for them to stop but they wouldn't let up. His blood was now smeared on the bathroom floor and I stood back with a smile on my face.

I was minutes away from getting physically raped and becoming emotionally damaged all because of a mother fucker who felt like women owed him something.

Seeing him on the floor crying for his life brought nothing but satisfaction to my heart. Once again, Carter came through and had my back like he always had.

IMANI

TWO DAYS LATER

*I*t was the first of the month and I was already running thirty minutes late. My voicemail was filled with messages from potential clients and this indeed was something big for me. Even though I worked alongside my cousin and his wife, I still needed to have something to call my own. I had plans on having my own business and office one day but I knew that I had to crawl before I walked. That's why I didn't mind taking things slow to learn everything that I needed to know about the business world before venturing out on my own.

I placed the key in the ignition and tried to start it but nothing. As always, I was out of gas again. Grabbing my purse and my phone, I rushed back into my house and slammed the door behind me almost dropping every decor off my wall. Once Latron jumped up from the couch, he knew he was in some shit when he saw the anger in my eyes. But knowing him, he didn't give a damn anyway and he was just full of the same excuses.

Every damn weekend he would take my car, run the streets, and bring my car back to me on empty. With no regard of me having to go to work during the weekdays. He was like a fly that

I couldn't get rid of, and because I allowed him to see my hand, I was stuck with him for the meantime. He had too much dirt on me, and I regretted it until this day.

"What the fuck, Latron! I have to go to work and my car has no damn gas in it. I'm already running late and you just lying there like it don't matter to you. When were you going to tell me? Thank God, the car didn't even start. It could've stopped on me while I was driving to work!" I snapped.

"Calm your ass down Imani! Just call that damn AAA Company and have them bring you some damn gas. You acting like it's the end of the world or some shit. Yeah, I didn't put any gas in it but I was too tipsy when I left the pool hall last night and I didn't want to make any stops. You know I ain't got no damn license. I was just trying to make it home to you. That's all."

"You just inconsiderate as fuck, Latron! It's nothing but the same damn excuse with you. When the fuck are you going to change? You know what... never mind."

I stormed out the living room, leaving him sitting on the couch with his head hanging low. Latron used to be so motivated and hardworking until he got comfortable with my hustle. He saw how fast the money was coming in and decided that he didn't have to work as hard anymore. Then when he found out who Carter was, he definitely didn't give a damn about making an effort to do a thing.

Every damn bill was on me and the biggest mistake I made was letting him in on all the dirt that I did. Every time I threatened to kick him out, he would throw it in my face about the things that he knew and I couldn't take that risk by letting him go out there to expose me. So I had to keep him close.

I tried to think of one hundred ways to get myself out of this situation without looking too suspect but nothing would ever come to mind. His friends and family knew where he stayed at even though they didn't care to visit. Also, there was no telling who else he told about my dark secrets. I didn't trust him or the damn people he kept around so I played it safe by tolerating him and allowing him to *think* that he was safe with me.

I closed the bathroom door, and with my back leaned against it, I broke down in tears. All I wanted was somebody to love and support me like I did them, but I was only getting the bitter end of the stick when it came to Latron. While all my friends were happily married or deeply in love with their boyfriends, I was busy taking care and babysitting a grown ass man who I didn't even want anymore. A man who I knew would never change because he was nothing but a leech, and he didn't see a damn thing wrong with being one either.

Not only was he a leech but he was a damn gambler and an alcoholic too. In my book, those were the two worst combinations that anyone could combine together. Latron was the reason why I didn't have any electronics in my house anymore and why I didn't buy any expensive décor for my place either. He was like a crack head and he would steal and sell any damn thing he could get back with money or liquor with. And each time I confronted him about the shady things that he did, it would just tell me the same tired ass excuse. He would make it seem like he was doing those things for us but it was obvious that it was for his own selfish reasons.

I could now hear him pacing back and forth in my bedroom and opening and closing the dresser draws. I knew exactly what he needed and was looking for: it was money. I blocked him out and slowly walked up to the mirror that was standing before me. I was disappointed at the woman that was staring back at me because I knew that I deserved better. I had bags underneath my eyes from many sleepless nights that I kept hidden with my favorite *Fit Me* foundation. Then some of the strands from my naturally curly hair were turning grey and I knew it was all because of stress and not because of my age. Luckily for the wigs that I wore on some days, I was able to keep those greys tucked away. Today, I just didn't give a damn, though. I looked exactly like what I been through, and I didn't give a damn about that either too.

I didn't understand why Latron treated me the way that he did because I was every man's dream. At least, that's what I thought. I was hardworking, loyal, and I kept up with myself like any woman should. My hair and nails were always done, hygiene was on point, and I made the 180 pounds that I carried around look real damn good. But in actuality, I was just a target for leeches like him. I was everything and more so that meant he didn't have to work as hard for me.

Tears kept running down my face as I thought about how much I hated him deep down inside. I knew that it was a terrible emotion to feel for someone but the love that I had for him dissolved a long time ago and I didn't know what else to feel for him but hate.

"Aye what you doing in there? I gotta holla at you right quick. Can you come out? I'm sorry about everything but I thought of something." He softly knocked on the bathroom door.

"Yeah! Give me a second." I huffed.

I took a deep breath and reached for my makeup wipes to remove the foundation off my face. Because of him I had to wash my face and reapply my foundation again because I ruined it with pointless tears.

After five minutes, my face was fit for work and I walked out of the bathroom like nothing ever happened like I always did. It was my weekly routine with him and I knew that crying meant nothing to Latron and that's why I did it in private away from him now.

He was now lying on my queen size bed like he was a king and that did nothing but piss me off all over again. I rolled my eyes at the sight of him and my stomach began to turn from being nervous. I couldn't wait for the day that he leaves my life for good because the evil thoughts that I was having about him, wasn't a good one and I was afraid of what it might lead to one day.

"Listen. Drew just called me, and he said that tonight is going to be jammed packed at the pool hall. I know for a fact that I can make that money back that I lost last night. All I need is a few hundreds, and I'm back on." He stood up to his feet and said with excitement.

"Yeah and when you lose a game, then what? You gonna call me to bail you out when those fools are damn near close to killing your ass because you can't pay up? I can't keep doing this Latron. I'm trying to take-off with this business, and I should be saving right now. Not investing into your bad habits or whatever else you have going on." I shook my head.

"What the fuck, Imani? Why it always have to be about you? I'm trying to do right by you and bring some money in this damn place and you keep talking about what *you* have to do! What about me? It's fuck me, huh?"

He was now hovering over me trying to scare me like he always did. With him being 6' 2" in height, I could feel every drop of spit landing on my face after each and every word that leaves his mouth. Not only did he try to intimidate me with his words but he used his height to do the same too. I was just hoping that we didn't get into any physical altercations because spring was slowly approaching and because of my light brown skin complexion, it would be hard for me to hide my bruises like I did during the winter.

"All I'm saying is that this is bad timing and I can't keep giving you free money when I have a load of stuff to do and bills to pay on my own."

I took a step back and once I saw the look in his eyes, I knew that whatever I said meant nothing to him. It was either I gave him what he wanted or he was going to take it from me anyway. Just like my car and everything else that he felt entitled too.

"I don't have time to play these fucking games with you and listen to you make excuses! I know you have some damn money. You always do!" He yelled.

He reached for my purse that I was still holding in my hand, and for a few seconds, we began to tug with it. Enough was enough, and at this point, I didn't give a fuck what he had to tell the world about me. I wasn't giving him another dime because this was my season to shine. I could feel it in my soul, and I wasn't letting anyone get in my way, especially not him.

"Let my purse go! I worked hard for my money and every damn thing that's in this place. You ain't put in on nothing in here. How dare you try to take from me!" I yelled.

His facial expression changed, because for the first time, I was standing up to him. For a whole year I allowed him to have his way and make non-stops threats to me. Today was his last day, and I was putting that on my daddy.

"You really consider yourself a hard worker after all the fucked up things you do to people? You ain't shit just like me so what makes you any better? People just don't know it yet and when they do, you gonna be out of luck." He laughed.

For the one second that I lost focus and allowed what he said to hit me personally, he pulled my purse from my hand and unexpectedly I fell on the floor hitting the back of my head on the wall.

"I HATE YOU! Get the fuck out, and I mean it. Get the fuck out. I never want to see you again!" I cried.

I rubbed the back of my head and watched as he removed my wallet from my purse and peeled off $500.00 from the wad of cash that I had. There was $2,000 sitting perfectly in my wallet that I was getting ready to deposit at the bank before noticing the car didn't have any gas in it. After working late the night from one of my other side hustles, I didn't have a chance to make a stop at the bank. Now I was kicking myself because I knew better than to bring anything home that he could take from me. I had plans with that money and just as always, he ruined it.

"Whatever you say! See you later." He stuffed the bills in his pocket and threw my wallet and purse at me and walked out the door.

"Laugh now and your family will be burying you later. Latron James Everson. I am going to make you pay," I said to myself.

❧

"GIRL WHERE THE HELL HAVE YOU BEEN? YOU HAVE THREE clients that have been waiting on you for at least two hours now. I tried calling you but your phone was going straight to voicemail," Kenya said.

"I'm sorry girl. Latron and I had a long night and you know how that goes. My phone died and I didn't even know it until he woke me up for breakfast this morning. Don't worry, I'm going to get them in and out in no time." I smiled.

"Yeah I know but you also know how your cousin Carter is when it comes to business. The last thing we need is people running their mouth out there and making us look bad," she said.

"I'm sorry, girl, but it won't happen again. I'll talk to him later too. Is he here yet?" I began to look outside of her glass office.

"No he has a few showings today so he won't be back until later around 4:30pm. Don't worry, I won't mention it to him. You just have to make sure that your clients walk out of here happy so they won't have to mention it to him themselves."

"You're right! Let me get to work."

Kenya turned her focus back on the computer and the second I walked out of her office, I called my first client in.

One thing I never wanted a happy bitch to see was when I wasn't happy. We couldn't relate, and at the end of the day, I would just be the topic to any happy woman's conversation. Latron wasn't shit and never would be. He could never compare to Carter. My cousin been a hustler since I could remember and even when my aunt kicked him out, he still was able to boss up from it. He never cried about it or ever hurt Kenya because of it. Meanwhile, I spent my life dealing with men and their anger, bitterness, and mommy problems.

Carter and Latron were in two different worlds and I could never share those horror stories with them. That's why I was busting my ass. I knew that one day I would find a man who was motivated like I was. I wanted to smile like Kenya and go to sleep at night with no worries like she did.

I deserved to be happy, and at this point, I was willing to die trying. Everything that was taken from me, I was going to get it back double, and I swear it on my life.

CARTER

"*A*re you sure that's what you want to do? You know once you open that door, it's not going to be easy to close that shit back up." Teddy advised.

"Trust me, I know. That situation been heavy on my mind all week and I just can't seem to shake it off. And to see her put in so many hours at the office and not getting any sleep when she's at home is fucking with me too. I know she's stressing about that shit. All she been doing is staying busy so she won't have to think about it but I know her. I just don't want her going into one of those depression modes and be all fucked up inside. I've witnessed that shit first hand before and it's not pretty." A memory of the past instantly came to mind and I closed my eyes trying to block those memories out.

Teddy and I went from working closely with each other on the streets to being the best of friends and business partners. When we decided to put the streets behind us and it was official between us. He wasn't just my old boss anymore but also my mentor aside from everything else. Whenever I had a problem whether it was big or small, I could always count on him. And when the numbers don't look right at the office, I would call on him to help me through it too. He was my mentor and financial advisor. He was the person who I trusted with my life aside from Kenya. The love and loyalty that I had for him was the same for him because he knew that I would put my life on the line for him like I had before in the past.

Teddy reminded me so much of my first mentor Mr. Clark who I had growing up minus the street life that he taught me about. Our bond was so tight just like it was with Mr. Clark. Mr. Clark saved me, and because of that, I owed him my life. When the money starting flowing in for me, I promised Mr. Clark that I would take care of him until I breathed my last breath. Since I made that promise to him, he never needed for nothing, and I was happy that I was able to pay him back for everything that he had done for me when I had nobody else to turn too.

Mr. Clark is now retired and living at home with no worries just like he always dreamed. His son, Brad, went off to college and since Mr. Clark felt like he did a great job with the both of us, he was able to sleep better at night now and that made me proud.

But Teddy, Teddy was my main man and everyone knew it. He gave up the game to the younger folks and I respected him for that. Shortly after, I followed behind him. He valued his life more than the streets and he knew that all money wasn't good money especially when it wasn't legit. The more I watched how he moved on a daily, the better man I became in my personal and professional life. I always followed behind him but today I needed him to ride with me on this one.

"Trust me. I understand how you feel but once we touch that fool, just know it's gonna bring a lot of heat out there. On the legal end, we can't afford to jeopardize our business and have it mixed up with the streets. But about Kenya, I would lay anyone down for her including you if you ever break her heart. We just have to be very smart about this there." He pointed at me.

"Listen, you never have to worry about that because I'm gonna guard her with my life. I made that promise to her the first week we met, and years later, ain't nothing changed. She could vouch for me on that." I pointed back at him.

Kenya and I had been riding together for so long that we could finish each other sentences, even when were not in the same room. And we were starting to resemble each other. There was no one I rather be with because the love she gave me every day proved to me that she deserved everything that I had to give her and more.

&.

"Now you boys know what to do, right? Let's make this shit quick and easy. Just in and out and there's no fucking around." I turned around and said.

After Teddy and I brief conversation earlier, it didn't take us nothing but twenty minutes to put our plan into effect. We made only one phone call and gave the green light. The fool that was responsible for causing Kenya's emotional distress wasn't too far from our old neighborhood which made getting in and out of the hood easier for us to maneuver around. He was slipping at a trap getting high as fuck so it was perfect timing.

But we had one minor problem and it was that Marquette was the nephew of one of our main business partners. Lorenz brought us a lot of business and I could've easily had a sit down with him about his nephew. But he knew me well enough to know that things were going to lead to more than just talking. By the time I would've had the opportunity to put my hands on Marquette, Lorenz would've had his nephew on the run somewhere and I couldn't have that.

When it came down to Kenya, there was no talking or understanding about anything with anyone about her. That's why Teddy was the only man who knew about my plans

70

because Kenya would've did everything in her power to talk me out of it. Teddy was down for whatever regardless of how I felt and that's why I had him here with me.

"Yeah we know boss man, this ain't our first run that we did with you." Joey laughed.

Joey was a jokester and that's why I said what I said. He didn't know when to take shit serious and I hated that. But he was a damn good shooter and that's why I kept him on payroll. As for Yung-G, he was the best of the best when it came to eating the streets up with his driving and the two together were fearless to many and unstoppable in the game.

Even though I had my crew there with me in order for me to keep my hands clean, I wanted to be there to witness Marquette taking his last breath. If we hadn't rushed in that restroom when we did that night, Kenya would've been a victim and that trauma would've ruined and scarred her forever. Regardless of the business relationship that I had with his uncle, I still had to do what I had to do because this shit was very personal to me, and there was no way of convincing me otherwise.

"Shut the fuck up with all that shit! You heard what the man said. Get in there, and make sure you don't fuck anything up or it's gonna be you that's looking down at the barrel of that gun. You feel me?" Teddy snapped and Joey got quiet because he knew that Teddy was serious.

When it came to Teddy handling business, he didn't joke about a damn thing, and that's why I loved when he was around.

I was more lenient than him and laid back. But depending on the situation like this one here, I could easily get on the same level as Teddy just like I was now.

The car was now silent and I looked at the faces of the two men and they were both calm and quiet. It was second nature for Yung-G to have a more chill personality. He didn't laugh, joke, or talk much about anything. It used to bother me until I realized that he was just about his money like Teddy and I was.

"Aight say no more! We'll be out in less than ten minutes. If not, y'all know what to do," Yung-G said.

Between Joey and Yung-G, Yung-G always took lead. He knew what to do and how to do it. He took orders without debating about it and wasn't scared to die if things unfolded and went left. Teddy and I both knew that if they weren't out in ten minutes, that we were going to have to jump in and get our hands dirty too. In past events, we never had to because we trusted their skills but regardless, we were always prepared for the worst.

"Aight, see you boys in five." Teddy dapped them up.

Teddy and I watched as the two grabbed their guns and hopped out of the car slowly walking down the block. We were parked in front of an abandoned house on the next block with the car running still. The trap that Marquette was chilling in was only three houses down. I watched as Yung-G and Joey walked in between two houses which we predicted would lead to the back yard of the trap and they could easily access it from there.

I exhaled deeply and titled my head back on the headrest because I wanted to be the one to put a bullet to that fool's dick. Marquette had violated Kenya in the worst way, and he was also known for being a hot-head in the streets. So, his actions didn't surprise me but he chose the wrong one to cross. Thanks to him, the shit he did just cost him his life, and whoever wanted to come after me because of it, I was ready for it too.

"Don't worry, you know they gonna handle up, right? There's no doubt about that. We been rocking with those boys since I could remember. They got this! Just sit back and relax," Teddy reassured me.

"Trust me, I'm not worried. I just wanted to be the one to put this gun down his throat and watch him suck on that shit. If we didn't run up on him when we did, God knows what would've happened to Kenya that night. That's all I keep thinking about." I held my gun up, turning it from side to side as I admired it while picturing what I wanted to do to Marquette.

"I know how you feel but that's what we pay those boys for so let them work. After we're done with this, Marquette is gonna be one less person that we have to worry about. It's that money season and we have to stay focus so let them handle that light-weight for you. We have bigger fish to fry. He just chose to dive in the wrong sea." Teddy laughed.

"Yeah I feel you, it's just…" I placed the gun on my lap and was surprised to see the person walking in front of the car as I sat up in my seat.

"Ahh damn… you want to step out and talk to her?" Teddy asked as he reached for my gun.

"Come on man. You know how I feel about all that. I'm not trying to get myself in that situation again. I just didn't expect to see her, that's all." I shook my head and turned away.

"I know how you feel but it's been a few years. I just thought…"

"Let's go!" Yung-G yelled when he opened the door and jumped in.

Without asking any questions, the second the both of them were in the car I slammed on the gas and sped down the block not looking back.

I quickly looked at them in the rearview mirror and could see the sweat dripping down their faces once they removed their mask. Their adrenaline was running and I knew that something either good or bad went down.

I made a few quick sharp left and right turns until I was clear from the block. I was now driving North on 7th Ave and felt a bit relieved when I didn't see any suspicious cars or police following behind us.

"Everything good? Y'all handle that or what?" Teddy turned in his seat to face them.

"Fuck!" Joey banged on the side of the door instead of answering the question.

"What the fuck happened back there? Y'all gonna speak or what?" I looked at them and they both avoided eye contact which was a bad sign to me.

"Listen, by the time we got there. That man was already dead. We don't know what the fuck happened back there." Yung-G looked up and answered staring me deep in my eyes.

"What!" Teddy and I said in unison.

"Just like it sound, boss man. He look like he been dead for only a few minutes though because his blunt on his ashtray was still lit. Nothing seemed out of place, not even the door locks. The doors wasn't kicked down or anything. As if whoever was there with him, knew him personally and just off him unexpectedly," Yung-G explained.

"Did anyone know y'all was going out there or did y'all hear anything about someone wanting his head too?" I finally drove up to a red light and I turned to look at the both of them.

"Naw, we didn't tell a soul!" Yung-G lifted his hands up.

"You don't even have to ask me cause I was ready to empty this clip inside of him. Like Yung said, we don't know what the fuck happened." Joey huffed.

"We'll let's get out the hood and we can figure this shit out later. Until then, no one speaks of this until we hear something first. Ain't no telling what beef he had out here on these streets. The only thing that concerns me now is if anyone saw you guys going in there. The last thing we need is someone holding us responsible for something we didn't get a chance to do ourselves," Teddy said, and we all nodded our heads in agreement.

The light turned green and I redirected my route and decided to get on highway 95 instead. I made a right turn at the light and a left onto the highway still paying attention to anything suspicious behind me. I now had a million things running through my mind and even though I shouldn't be driving, I needed to keep my mind busy.

I didn't want anyone seeing me zone out and going into deep thoughts especially Teddy. He had fucked my mind up just a few minutes ago and I was so close to snapping on him. He knew what I went through back then growing up in my momma's house and he thought I was supposed to feel sorry for her because she made it a priority to be a dope fiend.

A year after I left home, Mr. Clark told me that she started struggling with depression and she just gave up on everything including my brother Giovanni. Still having a heart back then, I reached out to her. I tried to comfort her regardless of the shit she had put me through because at the end of the day she was still my mother. I gave her a few thousands to keep in her pocket and so that she could catch up with bills. Little did I know that I was supporting a habit that she had no plans on running away from anytime soon.

When I found out about her drug addiction it broke me into a million pieces and like always, she disappointed me. She went from being depressed to chasing me down for money to feed herself that poison every day. A part of me felt guilty because it was the same product that I used to sell to someone else mother back then when I used to hustle on the block. Now I was living proof of my own karma and I had to accept that it was happening to me too.

But instead of being mad about the problem, I tried to get her help by helping her get into a program. When she found out what I was trying to do, she would go missing for days and weeks at a time. Far as Giovanni, he was not strong enough to handle her. He quickly got in contact with his father and went off to live with him and that was the last I ever heard from Giovanni.

Now years later and my momma was looking at least one hundred pounds lighter, dirty as if she hadn't showered in months, and lost with no sense of direction. Seeing her walk by in front of the car talking to herself and not even recognizing me, almost broke me inside again but I had to shake the feeling off.

I had to snap out of it because someone like her didn't want to be helped, and talking to her wouldn't change a thing either. I promised myself that I was not going to allow her to mentally drain me again. I had a wife and a business to worry about now. It's sad but I can't make her a priority because she never made me one.

Aside from that, I was now tripping and thinking about who could've been responsible for Marquette's death. Someone got there before us and even though Yung-G and Joey vowed that they didn't speak a word of our plan to anyone, I couldn't help but look at them a little sideways. With all that is going on, I just hope that I don't have to put a bullet in one of them for running their mouth about this. Not only would we have some street beef going but Teddy and I had our business to protect. We didn't need anything linking back to us especially when we weren't responsible for Marquette's death.

Thanks to the mother fucker who hit him first, we had some homework to do. If word got out about our involvement in any way, we not only was going to lose Lorenz as a business partner, but someone was going to die next over all of this.

KENYA

TWO MONTHS LATER

"What do you think about this dress here? I am stuck between the red and the black dress. They both look good as hell." I pointed at the dresses on the computer screen.

Carter and I were days away from celebrating our anniversary together and I wanted him drooling the second he saw me walk into the room with that body con dress on. We were finally over our busiest season in the year and it was time that we spent some quality time together. I just wanted us to have a nice quiet weekend together so we could get back to the money first thing Monday morning.

Every year, we would spend our anniversary turning up on someone's island right after we were done with the tax season but this year, he wanted to chill somewhere locally and I was okay with that. Carter had been walking around all tense lately and I could sense that he needed a break so it was perfect timing for the weekend that I was planning. Between the office work load, doing showings on a daily, and taking care of home. We definitely needed to spend some quality time together to get some of that load off.

"You know you look good in anything girl so it doesn't really matter." Imani was stuck on her phone and barely paying attention to what I was showing her.

`"Yeah, I know that. I'm just undecided that's all so I'll appreciate your opinion if you don't mind." I smiled to her.

"Well get the both of them then, that's my opinion! Ain't like you can't afford it though. You got it, so get it!" she said with an attitude.

"Hold up! What the hell is wrong with you? Somebody done woke up on the wrong side of the bed today I see. Are you okay? Because you really tripping over nothing right now."

I closed the screen on the computer and logged off to give her my full attention. Imani always had an easy-going, fun, and I don't give a fuck personality. To see her be on edge like this over nothing, I knew that something had to be wrong with her. The last time I ever saw her act like this, we almost went to jail behind it.

"There's nothing wrong with me. I'm good!" She dropped her phone on her lap and crossed her arms over her chest.

"Naw, it's *something* and you can't even lie to me. You almost took my head off over a damn dress. So what's going on with you sis?" I wrapped my arm around her hoping she would open up to me.

The second she felt my touch, I felt her body relax. She then bowed her head trying to hide the glossy look in her eyes. It was then that I knew that something was affecting her because this would be the first time that I actually witnessed her crying. I started to feel warm inside because I was getting emotional for my friend. We were so connected and that's why if she hurt, then I would hurt too and it was vice versa.

"I'm sorry about that. I fucked up on something and I wish that I can just talk about it but this is not the right time right now. It's hard to explain but..." She paused and that's when I noticed that tears were rolling down her face.

"Damn sis. What's wrong? Do we have to fuck somebody up or what? Because I can't see you like this. This is not you. Let me know what is going on with you, I don't care about it not being the right time. With tears rolling down your face, the time is obviously now." I leaned in closer to hug her tightly.

Unexpectedly she started laughing because that crazy shit is what Imani liked and what actually attracted us to each other. We didn't take shit from anyone and we were always down to ride for one another. The last time a man made her cry, he wasn't able to recognize his car after the damage that we had done to it.

If we had to set another example, I wouldn't mind locking up the office to do so. I could remember when I used to hustle back then before Carter and I become legit and changed our lives. Imani would just pick me up on the block and one day she saw me getting into a fight with someone who was trying to rob me. I don't know who sent him but he obviously didn't know anything about me. Well Imani hopped out of the car with a bat, we took turns beating ass, and ever since then Imani and I had been tight like crazy glue.

"No girl! We don't have to pull up on nobody. I'm just going through the motions, that's all. Just a lot been going on in my personal life, and when I'm ready to talk about it, you know you will be the first to know about it. I promise." She looked up and quickly dried her eyes.

I followed her eyes and saw that Carter, Teddy, and Yung-G had walked in the office and were talking in the lobby. I smiled to myself because ten years later, Carter still made my heart race every time I'd see his face. He was still the same man that I fell in love with back then, and that's how he was able to keep me on my toes. He never switched sides and remained loyal to me throughout the years.

"Well enough of all that emotional shit. There goes your man and his damn puppies following behind him like always." Imani smirked.

"She's back!!!" I laughed.

"What slick shit she done said now? I could see it in her eyes and I could tell that she was selling out," Yung-G asked once they all walked in my office.

"Mind your business damn! You just got here and ain't nobody was talking to you. You just want to seem important for once in your life." Imani rolled her eyes at Yung.

"Yeah whatever you say Imani... whatever you say." Yung-G winked at Imani and a took a seat in front of my desk.

Imani and Yung-G had been going at it for as long as I could remember. If you ask me, they act more like husband and wife than frenemies. They were alike in so many ways and that's why their personality always clashed. If you ask me, I prefer that they just be together and avoid all the dumb childish games already. It was obvious that they were into each other but with their pride and attitude, it was hard for them to accept and see the signs for what it really was. Regardless of Imani's current relationship, I still think that her and Yung would make a cute couple. They just don't know it yet.

"How you doing, baby? You gotta start learning how to ignore those crazy two love birds over there. They only gonna drive you crazy." Carter walked over to me and kissed me on my lips.

"I know right. I was sitting here trying to plan our special weekend getaway and here comes the drama between them. But you're right. I'll let them be."

"How you doing Kenya? How's business going?" Teddy asked.

"Business is going good as usual, you already know." I replied.

"Well let me get out of here before this fool start back up

with his foolishness again." Imani stood up from her seat with her purse and phone in hand.

"Actually, I'm right behind you. I have to pick up Layla from basketball practice in a few anyway. And it looks like it's about to rain so I don't want to be late." I stood up from my seat also.

"Hold up, what the fuck they want?" Yung stood up too.

We all turned our attention to the lobby and saw a few men walking in. Then when I read *FBI* written in a bright highlight yellow color on their jackets, I knew that something was up. I held a tight grip to Carter's arm once the airs on my skin stood up and that usually wasn't a good sign.

"Yeah, I wonder what the fuck they want?" Teddy said and opened the office door.

"We're looking for Carter Antwan Thompson, we have an arrest and search warrant," one of the agents said.

"How may I help you?" Carter asked.

My legs started getting weak and everything around me was becoming a blur. Within minutes, the office was filled with agents walking in and out with boxes in their hands. They confiscated all of our computers, laptops, and clients files that we kept stored in the cabinets. Everything we worked hard for was tumbling down right before our eyes and the sight of it took every last breath out of me.

Carter was pulled from my hand and instantly placed in cuffs. I couldn't move or speak and watching Teddy and Yung-G paced back and forth in the office was making me nauseous. Carter didn't say a word because he knew not too especially with our lawyer not being present. It wasn't his first time dealing with the law but definitely the first since we been walking a straight narrow for so long.

Nothing was making sense to me and I was in a state of shock. After hearing the word *fraud*, I went blank. My whole life was changing in front of me and the love of my life was also walking away from me for the very first time. Imani was standing and talking to me. I could see her lips moving but I couldn't hear anything that was coming out of her mouth.

She then pulled the seat from my desk and helped me to sit down. Tears started to roll down my face and when I realized that Carter was actually gone, I came back to reality. I looked around the office and exhaled deeply when I saw how empty it now was. Not only did the realization of our business just hit me but I knew for a fact that our accounts were frozen as well. Luckily for us, we kept a safe in our house because we always prepared ourselves for the worst. Carter and I came from nothing so we knew how to keep a stash on hand if whenever life decided to test and betray us.

"Can you get her something to drink? You're just standing there! She's in shock and the last thing we need is her passing out on us." Imani yelled at Yung-G.

"Kenya you're stronger than this! You hear me? I don't know what is going on but this will clear up very soon. Believe that! We had been on point for years and I think someone is just trying to fuck up our reputation or something. You have nothing to worry about. I will get down to the bottom of this so don't stress yourself out. Carter is strong and he knows how all this goes. Just give me some time, and I'll check on you later," Teddy said and stormed out of the office in rage.

Yung-G placed a cup of water in front of me and followed behind Teddy because he knew he had some work to do too. If Carter didn't have me, he knew that he could always depend on Teddy and Yung to have his back.

"Don't worry sis. Everything is going to be okay, I have your back like I always do. Carter ain't new to this like Teddy said. Trust me that whatever is going on, they will get down to the bottom of it. This too shall pass." I heard Imani say.

Still not being able to utter a word, I laid my head on her shoulder and cried like I never cried before.

KENYA

"*O*kay this is what we're dealing with right now. They currently have fraud charges against him. Some of y'all clients information were basically used to file false tax returns, order credit cards, and all kind of other stuff that I didn't want to hear about. It was anonymously reported and the feds picked it up and Carter's name is written all over it." Teddy explained.

Teddy had called me earlier and told me that he was stopping by the house after he left from seeing our lawyer. I wanted to be there with him but I knew that my heart couldn't take hearing any more bad news right now. I was still trying to digest what happened earlier and I was happy that Teddy and Yung decided to take lead and handle it themselves. Tomorrow was going to be a better day but as of right now, I needed some time to get my mind right and to think of what my next move was going to be.

"Okay so what now? Do we just sit and wait on a hearing date or what?" I looked around the room searching for an answer.

Teddy, Yung, and Imani looked at each other waiting to see who was going to respond first. I knew that they all were being cautious of what they say out of their mouths. It was a sensitive issue for me and I appreciated how delicate they were handling the situation.

"Yes we wait. I also told the lawyer to let Carter know that it is also best that he stays off the phones for now. As a result of that, we won't be hearing from Carter anytime soon. Not until his hearing date at least. Something doesn't seem right about all of this and I know that someone foul is behind it all. There's no way that Carter would jeopardize the business and do something as risky as that. Things not adding up and I could feel it in my soul that something ain't right about all of this." Teddy rubbed his hands together and I knew that he was thinking of a master plan.

He was right though. Carter had always been a hustler and he got everything that he ever owned by working hard for it. But stealing and defrauding people wasn't his thing. Like Teddy said, someone was definitely behind it and it was obvious. The sad part about the whole situation, we just didn't know who it was. We dealt with hundreds of people weekly and there was is no way of telling who the snake could be. It could be anyone from his past down to the present, we were simply in the dark and I hated that.

I just know that once I get my mental back that I was going to make sure that whoever was putting us through this, was going to pay us back with their life.

"Thank you, Teddy! I can't tell you how much I appreciate you. Once this day rolls over, I promise I'll be right beside you and Yung. I'm not gonna rest until we get that mother fucker. We all have to eat and I can't allow this situation to stop us from keeping money in our pockets. In due time, we will be back on though," I said.

"Don't mention it. We're all family, and we gonna be alright; believe that. We just have to stick together and keep everything confidential. Whatever the streets want to make out of this, let them. We have no control over what they're going to be saying out there but we can control what we say and let people know ourselves. I want y'all to stay off the phones and continue doing y'all regular and normal routines. Also, no posting none of that emotional and personal stuff on social media either. We can't let anyone see us sweat. Y'all hear me?" Teddy pointed at us.

"You don't have to worry about me, because I don't keep up with social media. So, I'm good on my end, and I have everything on lock including my lips. Now Imani? That's a whole different story. She posts her whole life on that mess. I don't know what she will do if that thing ever shuts down," Yung said.

"Boy, shut up! How you know what I post on my page anyway if you don't keep up with social media? Stalking much?" Imani snapped.

"Because you sit on your phone all day posting and it's not hard to read the word *Facebook* from your huge ass screen. You know I'm telling the truth." Yung laughed.

I shook my head because no matter what was going on. Whether it was a serious situation or not, those two always found the opportunity to jump on each other like two little kids. I definitely had to start doing what Carter told me and that is to ignore them at all times.

"Ok! Now that we cleared that up, I have to go and make sure that everything else is still up and running. I don't want anyone thinking that they could slack because one of our partners is not here. I'll check on you later., Teddy stood up and said.

I stood up and gave him a hug and Yung walked over to me and did the same. I felt some kind of relief knowing that I had a solid team behind me. Teddy and Yung were still holding things down for Carter, and Imani was by my side like she'd always have been.

"Again, thank you. I don't know what I would do without

you guys. Y'all support means a lot to me and I'm just happy that we are putting our heads together one this one," I said.

"Don't worry, sis. You're in good hands. In no time, we gonna be back on like you said," Yung said.

"Thank you, bro." I smiled.

They exited the house, and I sat on the couch next to Imani.

"Don't worry, sis. I'm not going anywhere. I'm just gonna go home and pack me a bag until you're ready to kick me out." Imani nudged me.

"I already know and I wouldn't let you leave anyway. I need my friend right now." I sighed.

"Hey Imani. How are you doing?" Layla walked in the living room and said.

"I can't complain. How you doing Ms. Super Star? How's basketball going?"

"It's good. I'm not a super star yet, but I'm learning a lot and having fun in the process too." Layla smiled.

Layla was so respectful, humble, and full of life. She had those same traits ever since she started walking and talking. To see her grow into a beautiful young girl made me proud. We only had each other growing up until Carter came in the picture and then it was us three. Carter and I did our best to protect and raise her the best way we knew how and looking at her now I can say that we did a damn good job. To see her be everything that we worked so hard for her to be, I couldn't be any happier. She stayed out of trouble at school, made good grades, and had a passion for basketball that no one could ever pull her away from.

I taught her to always put herself first, chase her dreams, and never give up. Each and every day she made sure she fulfilled those goals.

I promised her that as long as she focused on her goals that she would never have a need for anything in life. So far, she's been doing real good and it's helping me keep that promise.

"Well I like the sound of that so keep up the good work," Imani said.

"But I didn't mean to bother y'all but Kenya can I talk to you for a second?" Layla asked.

"Well I'm gonna let you girls have that sister-sister talk. I'll be back with my things and a bottle for us to sip on later." Imani smiled.

"Alright. Call me if you need anything," I said.

Layla followed Imani to the front door and locked the door behind her. I sat up straight in the couch anxiously waiting to hear what Layla wanted to talk to me about. We had such a good open relationship and she trusted me with her life. I always wanted her to feel comfortable talking to me about whatever was going on with her. I told her that no matter how young or old she is, I wanted to be the first to know everything about her and that made our bond even tighter.

I kept that bond with her because I didn't have that with anyone growing up and I didn't want her to go through the same things that I had too. I had to learn about life on my own and thanks to that I was able to discipline myself. I didn't let my experiences ruin me and I didn't put any of my hurt on Layla either. From my experiences and knowledge, I was able to pass it down to her and I was happy that I did.

Layla understood and respected my past and she never took advantage of it. And as she got older, she started to understand life herself and was handling it pretty well also.

"What's going on sis? Did something happen at practice today?" I asked her once she sat on the couch next to me.

"No… no… practice went well. I actually wanted to talk to you about *who* I saw at practice today." She winked at me.

I looked at her with a strange look as I tried to think of who she could be talking about. My mind was blank, and with Carter's situation currently taking over my emotions, I couldn't think of anything passed that and didn't want to work my brain either.

"Who? And please don't tell me to guess because my mind is going through too much right now and I can't deal. Just spill it."

"Yvette! That's who." She exhaled.

I was speechless because it had been years since we talked and seen Yvette. When Layla was eight years old, she asked to see our mother for her birthday and I had to respect her wishes so I took her to see her. Regardless of the personal feelings that I have towards Yvette, I couldn't keep Layla away from our mother because it wouldn't seem fair. I felt like, whether I had took her to see our mother or not, she would've either found her way or went searching for her on her own anyway. I had preferred to do it because at least I knew that Layla was going to be safe.

When we had showed up at our mother's place, she didn't even give us five minutes of her time, and she slammed the door right in our faces. Layla had ran to the car in tears and spent the whole night crying herself to sleep. I promised myself that I wouldn't allow that lady to hurt her like that ever again even if she begged to be in her life. Now to hear that she had shown up at Layla's practice was strange to me because she never showed an interest in wanting to see us before.

The streets talked and it's not like she didn't know about us or knew where we were. Teddy was a good friend of ours, so there was no excuse for her absence these past few years. We were financially stable, healthy, and we lived comfortably with no worries. If she was afraid of connecting with us back then, thinking we needed help or anything, she was wrong, because we were good and holding it down on our own without her.

Come to think about it, guilt or karma must've been kicking her ass. I don't know what the hell she would want with Layla at this point. Layla was underage and didn't have a thing to give her. If Yvette needed money, she was going to have to go through me which I doubt she would. I was too old for her to intimidate and make fake promises too. I hope she wasn't trying to scheme her way into Layla's life and break her heart again because I would definitely intervene this time around.

Then again, Layla was older now and could make the decision if she wanted that lady in her life or not. And if she wanted to give her second chance or not. Whatever Layla wanted to do I was standing behind her one hundred percent. No doubt about it. I just want to know what Layla's plans were because this was shocking to the both of us.

"Damn, I hope she's okay. It's kind of strange for her to just show up out the blue like that. Especially during one of your practices. That just means that she had been watching you for a while now and just never approached you but it was a good thing that you spotted her today," I said.

"Yeah I thought the same but she didn't look like she was dying or anything though. She kind of just sat there in amazement and I waited for her to approach me and she never did. I knew that I wasn't going to make the first move so I said forget it. Then when practice was over, she left without saying a word. As soon as I was getting ready to leave too, coach stopped me and handed me a note that Yvette left for me with her number on it." Layla pulled out her phone and showed me Yvette's number.

"Damn, that was brave of her. So what do you want to do? Do you want to talk to her?" I asked her.

The room fell silent, and Layla was now deep in her thoughts. I know that it had been a long time coming and she probably wasn't sure if she wanted to speak to her or not. From the last meeting, it had left her scarred. For her to make another attempt was going to be hard, but then again, the decision was all hers.

"At first I didn't want to but now I do. I just want to ask her one question. So, yes! I would love to talk to her but in person though. I need to look her in the eyes when I ask her what I've been holding inside for so long." She held the phone up and stared at Yvette's number.

"Okay, there you have it. Just send her a text message and set it up. The second she replies, we can head out there and you can get whatever it is that you have to off your chest." I leaned in and gave her a hug.

WE WERE PARKED IN FRONT OF A CREAM-COLORED DUPLEX THAT had three units attached to it. The duplex wasn't the best looking but it was an upgrade from the apartments that we grew up in back then. Just a few avenues away from our last apartment, we were about to meet our mother again after so many years, and I was just hoping that things went well.

"I texted her to let her know that we are here. So we just have to wait on her to come outside I guess." Layla shrugged.

I could see the excitement that she was hiding inside and I was just hoping that Yvette didn't disappoint her again. I had no feelings when it came to our mother because deep down inside, I knew that there was no fixing that. Some may say that I was wrong for feeling that way but I didn't give a fuck.

No one would ever understand what I went through and I didn't expect them too. For years, I learned to just be numb when it came to her. Her absence didn't bother me after a while. I trained my mind to just stay out of my feelings, and I blocked every memory of her out of my mind too.

Growing up, I had to do everything on my own for as long as I could remember. I learned to be very self-sufficient at a very young age, I matured quickly, and I walked around heartless. Those three qualities probably wouldn't have worked for some but I made it work for me. I was content with my situation at the time and whether Carter had come into our lives to save us back then or not, I was going to make a way for Layla and I regardless. That's why I didn't care too much for Yvette because I made a way out of nothing with no help from her.

"There she goes. Are you ready?" I pointed out the window.

Yvette stood at the top of one of the three steps and waved us in. What I thought was going to be a quick meet and greet was obviously going to be a long sit down between us. I wasn't ready to have a table talk about the past or our feelings because those things had got buried a long time ago in my mind right along with her.

Layla didn't even answer my question and was out of her seat belt and out of the car. I followed behind her and before I could even close the car door, Layla was standing in front of the yard staring Yvette deep in her eyes. Layla paid attention to a lot of detail and I knew that she was sizing Yvette down for answers. Trying to figure out who she was and paying close attention to her body language for any sudden changes that might throw her off.

Even though Layla received unconditional love from Carter and I, I knew that she still felt lost inside not knowing who she was. Yvette abandoned her when she was very young and she had no clue who her father was either. Her curly brown hair and light-skinned didn't match any physical features that Yvette carried so she was searching for answers. Layla wanted that missing piece to the puzzle in order for her to feel complete and I supported it.

The last time we saw Yvette, Layla didn't have the chance to interrogate her like she wanted too. Now that she was older, I knew that she was filled with questions that she needed answers too and I hope that Yvette was ready for it all.

"Hey girls! How y'all been? I heard that you guys are doing pretty good and I'm happy for y'all. Honestly, I am." Yvette opened her arms for a hug.

Layla looked back at me and I gave her a head nod. Once she

got the approval from me she walked into the yard and stopped when she was face to face with Yvette. Layla was staring her down, and after a few seconds, she finally gave in and accepted her hug.

As Layla embraced her, I stood back a few inches away watching her enjoy the moment with Yvette. The two of them started sharing tears and I felt happy for Layla because she needed that from her. She was still young and had a lot of questions floating in her mind which only Yvette could answer for her. Watching the both of them interact seemed so therapeutic, and I was happy that Layla got what she needed.

"Okay let's go inside before my nosy ass neighbors start poking their heads outside of their doors." Yvette opened her door.

We walked into apartment number two and I was amazed on how nicely decorated and clean it was. The smell of weed, ass, and sex didn't invade my nostrils like it used to when I was younger and that was a good feeling. The odor had stuck with me for so long that whenever I walked into a place that had at least one of the odors roaming in the air, it would instantly bring me back to my childhood and I would have to leave that location immediately most likely in tears too.

"Go ahead and have a seat. Do you girls want anything to drink?" Yvette asked.

"No thank you." Layla and I said in unison.

"Wow. I guess spending a lot of time together have y'all reading each other's minds too. That's incredible." Yvette smiled.

"Why did you let us go? Why didn't you come looking for us?" Layla interrupted and asked.

I sat back, waiting for Yvette to answer her questions because I wanted to know the answers too. Layla was still lost and trying to find herself. I was obviously doing the best that I could to keep her from dwelling over our mother, but in reality, she was still feeling empty inside; regardless of how much love I showed her.

"Listen, baby. If I could turn back the hands of time, I would. I was so young and stupid back then. Making excuses for myself and allowing the devil to take over my life with drugs, sex, and everything else that didn't consist of me raising my girls. I used to wake up every day kicking myself about what I had did to you girls, praying that I could turn back the hands of time. I say *used to* because I've made my peace with myself and asked God for forgiveness. Look at me. I got cleaned up, went back to school, and I am working now. I've built a relationship with God. I feel like my prayers have been answered because I prayed for the day that we all could sit down together and talk about this. I know that things won't happen overnight but I just need you girls to give me a chance to be in your lives again and with time forgive me for the things I have done. Momma didn't know any better and the only reason why I am still alive today is because of you girls. Kenya, I thank you for taking on the mommy role and holding things down. I know that it was a lot for you to manage at such a young age, but Teddy guaranteed and promised me that he would look after you girls and he did. Y'all are healthy and obviously turned out to be two beautiful and respectful young ladies. If anything had happened to y'all because of my wrongdoings, I wouldn't be able to live with myself. I swear. That's why I am thankful for this moment. I really am." She sighed.

I looked over at Layla, and she was in deep thought again. I wasn't sure what was going through her mind, but I knew that whatever it was she was searching on the right thing to say.

Yvette's little testimony was touching, but it was too late for me though. I wouldn't mind being cordial with her because I couldn't just forget about everything that had happened. And she was lucky that nothing didn't happen to us because she wouldn't have had the opportunity to sit down with us today to make her peace.

Teddy and Carter stepped up to the plate and played their roles very well. Not only did they have me to worry about but Layla was a toddler at the time too. She was only two years old but when we put our heads together, everything turned out better than expected, and we were able to live our lives with no worries after that.

Now years had gone by, and Yvette finally wanted to attempt to do right by us. I wasn't buying it, but if Layla wanted to, then it was all on her.

"What you thinking about, hunny?" Yvette leaned in and caressed Layla's lap.

"Nothing really. I just wanted to know what kind of mother would forget about her kids and then you explained what happened to you. It's no excuse though but hey, everyone's not perfect. If it wasn't for my sister, Teddy, and Carter, we wouldn't be here today. We probably would've been in the hands of the state while they bounce us around from group homes to group homes. I know all about it because a handful of my classmates are in group homes right now. Their moms gave up on them too, just like you did us. But to see you here trying to make an effort means a lot to me. I just hope that you are here to stay and not just trying to blow our heads up with fake promises. Kenya has always done right by me, and I won't ever trade her love and support for anyone else. So, are you here to stay or will you relapse and go back to your old lifestyle again?" Layla didn't bite her tongue, and that's what I loved about her.

I saw Yvette's eyes widened at the things that Layla said and I knew that it left her speechless. Layla was very wise and outspoken for her age and nothing could ever get passed her. She paid attention to people's vibes, body language, and she was big on energy. I don't know where she picked it all from but I was happy that she did because she definitely had characteristics of a leader and not a follower.

"Of course baby… of course. I am here to stay and y'all never have to worry about me leaving ever again. This is my place and whenever you and your sister want to come by and visit you can. I don't do any drugs anymore and I don't keep any friends around that don't mean me any well. I just simply go to work and back. If you have to test me out, you can. I have all the time in the world and I am willing to do whatever I have to in order to gain y'all love and trust back. I owe you girls that much so it's y'all call." Tears started to roll down her face again.

Layla stood up from the couch and so did I. I honestly was ready to wrap things up and was just waiting on Layla to make that exit. The tears didn't mean anything to me and I can tell that Layla didn't want to fall for it either.

"You don't have to cry because I forgive you. It will take some time but I am going to give you a chance because there's a lot that I don't know about myself and you are obviously the only one who can fill that void. I have your number so I'll keep in touch with you." Layla smiled at her.

"Thank you baby… thank you. I love you girls so much. I'm going to show y'all how much I've changed. I promise and you girls won't regret it." She stood up and walked over to us and gave us a bear hug.

I stood in place and didn't hug her back because I was emotionless. All I was able to do was spread a fake smile across my face and nothing more. Layla wasn't too much into the hug either especially when she noticed how stiff my body was. I didn't want to get my hopes up. But for Layla I was willing to give Yvette an opportunity to show Layla of the changes that she made.

Now that Layla was able to get that off her chest, I knew that she was feeling a little bit more relieved. She always wanted to know about her past and what happened with our momma back then. Because it wasn't my place to say, and I didn't want to put Yvette in a bad light, I always told Layla that her time would come when she would be faced with the truth, and Yvette would be the one to tell her. Today was that day, and I was happy that she waited because there was nothing better than hearing someone's story from themselves.

"Well, Layla. Go ahead and wait in the car. I'll be right there. Give me a few minutes with Yvette." I handed her the car keys.

"Okay. Well I'll give you a call later Yvette. It was nice seeing you." Layla waved and walked out the apartment.

"It was nice seeing you too, baby." Yvette waved.

Layla was very respectful, and I never had to repeat myself twice. I wanted to get some understanding with Yvette and Layla instantly picked up on that too.. Layla was like my child, and no matter how old she gets, I was going to protect her until the death of me, and I didn't care who didn't like it. Regardless if Yvette was our mother or not, the same rules applied to her also.

"I really want to thank you for bringing her here to meet me again. It means a lot to me, and I could tell that you did it for her too. Even though I know that we don't see eye to eye right now, I'm gonna make things right between all of us soon. Trust me! I can't get that time back, but I can sure enough make up for it," she said.

"Honestly, I don't care if you ever make things right with me. I'm twenty seven years old now and married. All I care about is Layla's heart, and if you break it, I promise you won't ever see us again. Trust me!" I answered rudely.

She was so stuck on patching things up with me, and I was more concerned about keeping her the fuck from around us. We were definitely on two different pages, but in due time, we will see if she really changed or if this was all an act. As of now, I wasn't going to put all of my eggs into one basket with her.

"I know that I've caused you a lot of pain but you have to let that hurt grow. You're still young, beautiful, and intelligent. Don't add hurt and bitterness into the mix. It won't do you well. Trust me, I know. I've been there and done that and I did all the wrong things because I was hurt and bitter. I'm just trying to do things right this time around while I'm still alive and able to do so. You can go ahead and get all of that out of your system now because you are going to see my face a lot for now on."

"Yeah, if you say so." I rolled my eyes.

"Also before you leave. I just want you to know that if you need any help on finding out who set your husband up, I got you. I may be working in my profession now but momma still the same old-g. My street creditability will never go away and once I put my head out there, that situation will be dead ASAP. You just say the word." She said with a serious face.

"Ok thanks. We'll be in touch." I nodded my head.

I walked out of her apartment trying to catch my breath because she was right. Everyone from the hood fucked with her and respected her regardless of the shit that she used to do. She was hustling like them so they didn't judge her. And if she knew about Carter's situation, I knew that her ears were still open in the hood. This door that I was about to open with her was going to bring out so many emotions, and I don't know if I am ready to handle it. She was not only willing to build a bond with Layla and I but also help me find out who framed my husband. I don't know what God is trying to show me, but I am definitely taking it as a sign.

IMANI

"*A*hh shit! Fuck me harder. Damn, that's all you got? You been talking shit all week," I demanded.

"Don't worry, I got you! I was just taking things slow but I didn't forget about the shit you been talking. All you did was make things worst on yourself." He gently wrapped his hand around my twenty-six inch Bohemian curly lace wig and pulled it back.

I bit down on my bottom lip and closed my eyes as I felt him pounding me with every inch that he had. With each stroke, I felt like I was about to release my juices on him but I was holding back because it felt so good. He gave good dick and I could never deny that regardless of how crazy I acted in public around people. I knew my ways bothered him at times though but it was the only way that I could get him to stay on his toes about me. I wanted him to stay focus, consistent, and of course only be fucked up about me. I had him where I wanted him and that's all that mattered.

Our weekly meetups started off on just the business tip and after one tipsy lunch date, he was in my guts and had been ever since. I couldn't lie though, he was the best that I ever had but I would never admit that to him. He satisfied me in every way possible to the point that I didn't even have to instruct him on what to do.

He took his time to learn my body and once he mastered the skill on how to please me mentally and physically, I had been head over heels about him like no other. Even after we settled our business agreement, I still had plans on keeping him around. Deep down inside I knew that we would take over the world together. As good as he was to me I wasn't going to allow another woman the opportunity to enjoy him the way I did. He was mine and once everything falls into place, I definitely wasn't going to let him go. I had true intentions and I wanted him to see that.

"Damn girl! This pussy is so damn good. I don't know why you kept it away from me for so long. All that playing hard to get shit and you keeping something as good as this to yourself." He moaned into my right ear making my nipples poke out at the sound of his voice.

Chills ran all through my body when I inhaled the mint Colgate smell from his breath. Even after he devoured my pussy into his mouth, he was still smelling minty fresh and it drove me crazy.

"I know what I have between my legs and that's why I have you crying in this pussy now." I smiled to myself.

He loved when I talked my shit during sex because I could feel the excitement running through his dick. The pulsating sensation let me know that he was close to reaching his peak as his pace picked up. I exhaled slowly and prepared myself for what was next.

Before I could even think more about it, he pushed my head into the pillow and spread my ass cheeks wider. With one hand on the headboard and both of his feet planted on the bed, he pounded my pussy with deep strokes almost causing me to gag like always. I was so used to it now that it didn't even bother me like it used too. When he used to share his desires with me and one was about him liking it ruff, I thought it was nothing that I couldn't handle.

Our first two times of doing it, I almost cried. Then I learned how to exhale, relax, and enjoy the penetration. In my mind, I knew that it wasn't going to last long, but with every stroke, I felt like my soul was about to come out of my body.

He dug deeper into me and now had his hand wrapped around my neck.

"Fuck... fuck... fuck... Ahhh... shitttt!" He yelled and banged on the headboard.

He gave me his last few pumps then pulled out and released all his seeds on my ass smearing it with dick as if he was painting a canvas.

Once he rolled over and laid on the bed beside me, I quickly turned around on my back trying to catch my breath. We were on round three and he was wearing me out because he saved the last round for him. He always focused on pleasing me first and that's why I allowed him to do what he wanted to do to me when it was his turn.

I knew that I was in for it the second we got behind closed doors because I had been selling out to him all week. Whenever I talked my shit or made him feel small, like he would say, he would get his revenge by fucking me how he wanted. He didn't care if I was struggling for air or not.

"Not to ruin the moment, but we need to talk? I had this on my mind all damn day, and I can't shake it off." I sat up in the bed facing him.

"Okay, what's on your mind? What do you want to talk about?" He reached for the towel on the edge of the bed and handed it to me.

"For one, we need to talk about the whole situation. I was all smiles when Teddy mentioned the charges that the feds had on Carter. How the feds said that his name was written all over that case indicating that they didn't suspect that anyone else was involved. When he said that, my whole world had lit up, because I felt like we were getting close. Then when he said that he wasn't buying it and convinced Kenya to feel the same way too, I knew that his ass was about to be a pain in our ass. That damn Teddy always had to put his two cents in things that didn't even concern him. Just the thought of him having his nose in this was about to make things harder than it needed to be, and with Carter not around, Kenya was definitely going to depend on him for guidance. Fuck!" I snapped and tossed the towel on the floor.

From the very first day that Carter introduced me to Teddy, there was something about him that I didn't like so I never cared for him. But because he was the one putting money in our pockets, I kept my opinions to myself and just went along with everything. As time went on I realized that Teddy was arrogant, bossy, and expected everyone to bow down to him because he fed damn near the whole hood. He was well respected in the city by residents and even law enforcement. Most of the officers who patrolled the hood grew up with him so they didn't fuck with him.

Those officers chose to change their lives and make something out of themselves while Teddy went the other route. Regardless of their different life goals, those officers still respect the street code and always looked the other way when it came to Teddy. He felt untouchable and actually he was.

He also had Carter running around the city like a damn slave being his do-boy and that was another reason why I didn't respect him. Carter was too young and blind to see it back then that Teddy was just taking advantage of him. I knew that deep down inside that Teddy didn't care for me either because he knew that I could see right through his greedy and selfish ways.

To avoid bumping heads with him, I stayed close to Carter. I used to make a few runs and pickups with Carter whenever he asked for me to be the driver because I didn't mind. And whatever Carter profited from everything, he always made sure that I got half. It wasn't anyone's decision or mine, it was Carter's. He was loyal as fuck to me until he started to let Teddy take over his mind and that's where the problem started.

Teddy convinced him to only hustle with strangers and not family because it gets complicated when money was involved so without asking me how I felt about it first, Carter instantly cut me off. Leaving me broke and trying to figure things out on my own which had me struggling for a while.

I didn't get any support from my immediate family because they acted like I didn't exist. Carter was my only hope, and because he allowed Teddy to ruin him, he caused me to build a hate inside my heart for him.

Years later when Carter became older and wiser, Teddy and him decided to retire from the streets and go legit. They opened businesses with their dirty money, and things had been great for them ever since.

But the guilt and rumors in the streets about me struggling, was eating Carter inside out, so he had no choice but to pity me and put me on. If it wasn't for the streets coming close to sabotage his name for shitting on his own family, he would've left me for dead.

Adding me to the team made a difference but not a big one. He was bird feeding me and I didn't like it. I wasn't making the salary that his wife and him were making and I needed more.

I got more *inquiries* about people wanting to clean their credits than clients actually paying me to do it. I spent so much money taken up those courses and I still couldn't make a decent check.

The most clients I had in a month was two and they didn't even finish out their six month contract with me. Once their score got to where they needed it to be, they canceled their membership which put me back to square one.

Carter was also dipping into other things which I knew for a fact that Teddy and him had partnered up on. The fact that Kenya was acting like she was oblivious to what else he had going on, pissed me off even more. They were bringing in more money than what they allowed me to see and that's why I had to take matters into my own hands.

"I wouldn't worry so much. Teddy just being Teddy. You have to remember. That man had been hustling since he was ten years old and he don't trust a soul. He witnessed so much growing up and that's why he is the way that he is. I'm not intimidated nor worried about him because all that macho shit is just a front. You just have to stay focus and keep doing what you're doing. Trust me things will work out real soon. We just have to be patient, that's all." He started caressing my back.

"I understand that but I just wish that we could get rid of him. I don't like how he is trying to take control of this situation especially when Kenya is in the dark right now. The more he comes around her, the quicker she will start to peep things like him, and we can't afford that. Teddy wants to be on top of things and looking through every crack for any possibilities and suspects. The only downfall to this is that they *really* know who Carter is. They know for a fact that he wouldn't scheme like that because that's not his hustle. Now they are going to work overtime trying to figure out who is behind it all and that only puts us in a risky situation."

"You are worrying too much, like I said. Right now you're taking the first step by spending more time over there with her. The more you talk to her and pick her brain, the more you will know about what's really going on. You can also find out if they have anything stashed in their house which I highly doubt that they do. We gonna need every dime. Also when Carter starts calling her, you need to be there listening in on all those calls too. It's too early for us to quit now. We're almost there. I know it seems like a lot but that's how it is. You knew from the beginning that it wasn't going to be easy. Don't break on me now. Listen, with all that shit that we planted on him, ain't no way those crackers are going to let him out that place. Their business and the office is on standstill and soon it will be down for good. When everyone in the streets finds out that they're fraud because they will, we will open up our own real estate company and be right on top like they were." He preached.

I smiled as I listened to him go over our plans like we had talked about before and it sounded so good and refreshing to be reminded of it again. He was right and I knew that this wouldn't be easy before I convinced him to carry out my plan. I knew that I was going to have to deal with the emotions, betrayal, and the risk. I had been broke for so long that I didn't even give a fuck who I hurt at this point. Family or not, I wanted to be rich.

Like he mentioned, we just had to patiently wait for everything to fall apart for them and fall into place for us then we would be right on top like we planned. I had all of their client's information and could easily contact them and promote our new business to them when the time comes. I was tired of struggling and making pennies while I watch Carter and Kenya go on their lavish trips and expensive shopping sprees like nothing else mattered to them in the world. It was my turn to be happy and I didn't care what I had to do or who I had to cross to get it. With my sweetheart by my side, I knew that we were going to live our best life together and I couldn't wait.

"Yung! I swear you're a genius and I'm so happy that we are in this together. Had I known that you had a mind like mine we could've been smashing goals a long time ago. All thanks to you right now, I am starting to feel better about this again and confident. Thank you baby!" I pushed him back on the bed and sat on top of him smiling from ear to ear.

"I told you before that you have nothing to worry about. We gonna both get what we deserve and in due time, you won't have to lift a finger. We can let the money work for us while we take trips, shop, and do everything that we wanted to do. It's going to get better, baby. I can feel it." I felt his dick rising up again and I knew that I was in for another hot and steamy round with him.

"You're right about that. I can feel it too." I winked.

He winked back and grabbed his dick, then I slowly went down on it, moaning the sounds that he loved to hear. Yung was everything in one, and I couldn't believe that we never made it happen between us. Not only was he good in bed, but he had a master mind. He was confident, energetic, and strong. I really had *lucked* up with him, and I couldn't wait until I enjoyed him without hiding to do so.

Latron's bum ass was one step from being tossed out, but thanks to Yung, he kept me calm through the storm. If I was Latron, I would have a plan in effect now because he was in for a rude awakening.

I closed my eyes and started slowly riding back and forth on Yung's dick as I thought about the storm that Carter and Kenya were about to face. Yung and I were going to take over the city of Miami and be rich forever. The two were about to finally know how it feels to be on the bottom like we were.

KENYA

*T*ears welled up in my eyes as I replayed the look that Carter had in his eyes when we were inside the courtroom. He was strong but yet I knew that he was feeling weak for me like I was for him. The only thing that gave me strength was the confidence of knowing that he was innocent. Also, the support team that I had standing behind me also assured me that regardless of how bad things may seem, that everything was going to be okay with time and patience.

Through his whole hearing, Carter was trying his best not to show any emotion so we wouldn't stress out once we leave. His bond was denied and that fucked our whole mood up. The Feds did everything they could to make Carter appear in a bad light. They brought up two of his past juvenile offenses that he had, which was irrelevant to what was currently going on if anyone asked me.

Carter spent years running away from his past and so did I. We worked hard on getting that old hood lifestyle image of us out of people's heads but once a person earned their streets creds, it was hard to do. We wasn't proud of the things we did back then because we were basically just trying to survive. Now it seems like all of our hard work and dedication of trying to change and be great in life didn't matter to those folks. I was frustrated beyond the belief but I knew that I had to stay strong.

I looked around the room and even though everyone had a clueless look on their faces, I was still happy to be surrounded by so much love and support. Even the person who I least expected was here with us to and that was Yvette.

Surprisingly, Yvette kept her word so far and had been working on her relationship with Layla and me. It was actually more so with Layla because I was too busy trying to put the loose ends together about Carter.

I didn't mind her though because Layla at least had someone to keep her busy while I worked and figured things out on my end.

"Is there anything else that you need me to do before I head on out?" Teddy asked.

"Naw you did enough for today by just showing your support. It means a lot to us. I just wish that I could sit on the phone and talk to him, you know." I sighed.

"I understand but the less that is being said on the phone, the better. Maybe Carter knows something that we don't and we don't need him giving out any hints over the phone. We just have to let the lawyer do his part at this point." Teddy instructed.

Carter and I talked about everything and never kept secrets. I just couldn't imagine that he knew who was behind all of this because that shit would crush me. Then again, he probably would keep that kind of information away from me if he was trying to protect me. Teddy also knew him better than I did so it was only right that I allowed him to lead for now and take his advice on everything. Teddy had served federal and state time back in the days so he was very much familiar on how everything works.

This was definitely the moment for me to trust the process and to work on being patient because I had nothing else to do.

"Yeah, I guess so. I was feeling optimistic until I went into that courtroom and heard all of the things that they were saying about him. Regardless, if this is a short or long ride I'm riding for mine.

"There you go! Don't let them break you or see you sweat. They get paid to do that shit and we just have to be ten steps ahead of their tactics. That's all."

Teddy stood up from the couch and I knew that his time was up. He could never stay somewhere for too long. The longest he ever sat around and talked to Carter and I was probably thirty minutes. That was only because we had a client in the office who was an old friend of his and they were catching up.

Teddy had this theory that sitting around and talking all day never got things done and people miss out on a lot in life because they didn't stay proactive during the day. He didn't know what a break or a vacation consisted of.

While Carter and I used to be on our trips living it up, you could always find Teddy in his office grinding or at home on the computer doing the same.

"Alright Yvette. Now you keep your eyes on my girls. I don't care how grown they think they're. Stay on top of them." He winked at Layla and me.

I shook my head because that was one of his favorite lines. To Teddy, I was still that little girl in his eyes who he helped raised along with her sister. At first it used to frustrate me on how protective he was but as I got older, I knew that he meant no harm and we were basically all he had.

He didn't talk about his family, having any kids, or even past or current girlfriends. Teddy knew more about all of us than we knew about him. Come to think about it, I wouldn't be surprised if his name wasn't even *Teddy*.

"I'm here, ain't I, and trust me, I got them. I wasn't on my shit before but I got them now. They won't regret this," Yvette said.

I looked at the both of them hoping that they weren't going to cause any feuds but they appeared to be pleased with each other. Teddy nodded his head and then walked over to Yvette to hug her.

"Alright y'all stay safe and call if anything and I mean *anything*. I don't want a damn thing going unnoticed that we let slip up." He pointed at us.

"Say no more."

Teddy walked out of the living room and the second he opened the front door, I heard Imani's voice booming through the house. She was loud at times and that's one thing Teddy didn't like about her. It was obvious that they didn't like each other but they had no choice but to deal with each other because of Carter and me.

"Who the fuck is that walking in here all loud and shit?" Yvette asked in a low tone.

"Yvette chill... That's my best-friend Imani. She's also Carter's cousin, so I consider her family. She said she was going to be stopping by the second we left court because she had some things to take care of this morning," I explained.

"So what? She's your *best-friend* ain't it? Her ass should've been in court with you today. Busy or not! Everyone else was there playing their part. There's no excuse." Yvette snapped.

"I understand what you're saying but..."

"Heyyyy, y'all! What's going on? How was court today, sis? Sorry I missed him but you know I had a lot of things to handle." Imani walked in the living room and said.

"Hey, Imani!" Layla sang.

"My man still ain't out so there's nothing to say about court. It's just the waiting game right now. What's going on with you though?" I gave her a dry answer because I wasn't in the mood to talk about it anymore especially after the little back and forth that Yvette and I just had.

"Sorry to hear that but I'm there at the next court date. You can believe that! Oh I'm sorry, I see that you have company today." Imani stared Yvette up and down and Yvette did the same.

The both of them had strong personalities. I was just hoping that they didn't clash. Imani wasn't scared to let anything come out of her mouth, and neither was Yvette. Imani was basically a younger version of Yvette and if I don't separate the two fast enough, one of them or maybe the both will be sitting their ass in jail too. With everything that was still pending with Carter, I couldn't add their drama on to my list right now.

"Oh yeah my bad. I can be so rude sometimes when my mind is busy thinking about a lot. I apologize but Imani this is Yvette. She's our... she's our mother. Yvette this is my best-friend Imani the one who I was telling you about before she walked in." I looked between the two and pleaded with my eyes hoping they got along.

The room fell silent and the both of them were reading each other debating on who was going to open their mouths first and say the first words. I knew exactly what kind of thoughts were running through Imani's mind because our bond was that thing. As for Yvette, I was lost. It had been so long since I've lived in the same household as her and even be around her. Yvette obviously changed throughout the years which I wasn't sure if it was a good or bad thing yet.

Throughout Imani and I's friendship, I never really opened up to her about my past. She knew whatever she knew because she got it from the streets but nothing directly came from me. Looking at Imani's facial expression, I could tell that she wasn't too pleased with Yvette.

Regardless if I had decided to tell Imani what I wanted her to know about Yvette, it wouldn't had changed anything at all.

That night that Layla and I got kicked out back then, Imani and Carter were the ones to rescue us. It didn't take a college degree to figure out that Yvette was a no shit ass momma. And whatever the streets told Imani, made Yvette look even worst in her eyes. Imani didn't bring her up in conversation just like I didn't so that confirmed to me that she didn't have any respect for Yvette.

I never argued or stressed my concern to Imani about Yvette because there was nothing that I could do about it. Yvette was whoever she was and I didn't care to get in the way of her karma because I knew it was coming.

Now that Yvette is here without knowing her full intention, I had to sit back and monitor her like a close enemy. I just hope that Imani doesn't get in the way of that.

"Well nice to meet you. Glad that you could *finally* join us after the long dreadful day that we had at court today." Yvette smirked.

"Excuse me! Did you just say *finally*? Well, I should say the same about you because you had been gone so long that we didn't even think that you still had a pulse," Imani fired back and laughed.

I shook my head from side to side and Layla sat in the couch with her mouth wide open in amazement. As much as Layla and I was hurt because we had to grow up without a mother, we still couldn't find it in our hearts to disrespect Yvette.

Far as Imani, she was just a different breed and I'm sure that she felt like she didn't owe Yvette a damn thing. She didn't care to hold back her feelings and if she continued talking, there was no doubt in my mind that she couldn't kill Yvette with just words.

"Listen little girl! I am old enough to be your damn mother so tone that shit down. If you think for once that I have to explain or answer to you, you have this all fucked up. I'm just here for the two people that I owe my life to and no one else! So fuck what you heard about me and let's talk about who I changed to be. Deal?" Yvette stood up from the couch and voiced.

If looks could kill Yvette would've been dead because Imani was fuming with rage. I could hear Imani's breathing from where I was sitting and I noticed that her hands were beginning to shake.

Now I was regretting that I didn't call Imani earlier to tell her that she should stop by later. Having Yvette here was bringing on mixed emotions for her and I didn't expect her to understand Layla and I's situation.

Layla wanted closure and wanted to move on in life. She wanted to brush up on her relationship with Yvette and whatever she wanted to do, I had to be down to do it too because it has always just been Layla and I.

"There's no deal! I just hope that your ass is here to stay and not coming to leech on to any of them. But just like you don't have to explain a thing to me, I don't need to sit here and deal with you also."

"Sounds good to me!" Yvette smiled.

"If you need anything Kenya, please call me to let me know! And when you do, just make sure that your so-call *mother* is not around when you do. I would love to stay but I'm good. This room is just too crowded for me right now." Imani's voice started to shake, and I knew that she was officially pissed off.

"I'm sorry but yeah, it's best that I call you later," I said.

"Yeah see you later. Hopefully, you show up this time." Yvette laughed.

Imani rolled her eyes and made her way back out the front door without defending herself. If Yvette knew Imani like I did, she would've shut her damn mouth. Imani had a short fuse and anything gets her going. I exhaled deeply the second she made the initiative to turn her back and walk away. I knew it was something hard for Imani to do because she never missed an opportunity to slap her a bitch.

In a way I was kind of happy that Yvette stood her ground too. For the first time ever, she proved to us that she had our backs and was letting anyone get in the way of being there for us.

"I'm sorry about that but Imani just really cares about us. She had been there for us since day one and she's very protective of who comes around us. I can't say that's she's right but you have to understand why she feels the way she do. You being here just doesn't sit well with her knowing what she knows," I said.

"Yeah. Imani is family Yvette and she always had our backs. She's like an aunt that I never had. She used to babysit me and all when Kenya was at school. So, it would be nice if you would apologize to her when you can," Layla said.

We both looked at Yvette, and she had a blank expression on her face. I didn't care who was going to be the bigger person, but someone was going to have to. Especially if Yvette had plans on staying around for good. She was going to have to make it a priority to get along with Imani.

"Maybe I was wrong for how I came at her and should've kept my opinion to myself, but I couldn't. I could see right through that girl and I don't trust her. I respect the fact that she held y'all down when I didn't but that still doesn't do anything for how I feel inside. The second I heard her voice and seen her face, I could tell that's an angry jealous ass woman. She may have y'all fooled but not me. I dealt with women like her for years and could read them from a mile away. Watch what I tell you," Yvette said.

I was speechless. I never thought Imani would be jealous of anything. Angry? Yes. But not jealous.

She was in our circle making money just like us. She had no kids, no drama, and lived comfortably like we all did. Imani had no reason to be jealous of me or anyone in our circle. But that was just Yvette's personal feelings about her, and I wasn't going to let that change how I feel about my friend.

"Just give her some time and she will grow on you. For now, I just need for y'all to make peace and get along. If you plan to stay for the long run like you say. I need you to do that for us. We have enough going on right now and I can't be worried about breaking up fights between two grown women," I said.

"Respect, but it still doesn't change how I feel about her though. But for you girls, I'll be on my best behavior. That doesn't mean that I won't have my third eye on her. It's something about her, and I just don't trust her," Yvette said.

"Well that's good enough for me. What about you, Layla?"

"Yeah, it's good enough for me too. I just don't want y'all fighting. You know?" Layla said.

"Yeah, I know, but forget all that. Anyway, before your friend came walking in with all that noise. I wanted to tell y'all that I have a surprise for the both of you. And please don't ask me what it is. I just need for y'all to agree to come with me and see it. Y'all won't be disappointed. I promise," Yvette said.

"Are you down for a surprise?" I asked Layla.

"Of course!" She smiled.

"Okay cool. Let's see what you have waiting on us." I shrugged.

KENYA

$\mathcal{W}$e were now parked in the Wells Fargo Bank parking lot on 7th Ave waiting on Yvette to pull up. I told her that it was best that we drove in separate cars. I had a full day of errands in front of me and I didn't want to delay them. Layla also had a scheduled lunch and movie date later with her two best-friends and she didn't want to be late to that either.

Aside from the surprise that we were patiently waiting on Yvette to reveal, I had a love letter sitting in my purse that I couldn't wait to pull out and cuddle in my bed with and read. Before I left the courthouse earlier, I rushed to the restroom to wash my face from all of the anxiety that I was experiencing. I felt like I was seconds away from passing out every time someone opened their mouths in that damn room. They weren't saying a damn thing that I wanted to hear and I didn't know how much longer I was going to be able to take anymore.

When I reached for a paper towel to dry my face, a female correctional officer walked in and approached me as if she knew me personally. She then placed the letter in my hand giving me a small squeeze and quickly walked out without saying a word. Afraid of anyone walking in behind her, I stuffed the letter in my bra and walked out with a smile on my face because when it finally hit me, I knew that the letter was sent with love.

In my heart, I knew that there was no way that Carter was going to allow another court date to go by without us exchanging some type of communication between us. I could see it in his eyes that he had so much to say to me. I was feeling the same way too.

He understood the restrictions that we set for ourselves though and I couldn't do anything but respect it as well.

Even though I know that after reading his letter that I wouldn't be able to reply to him, I just felt so loved and special that he made an effort to comfort my heart. I didn't have to say too much and he knew exactly what my heart needed for the meantime.

"What do you think she has to show us?" Layla interrupted my thoughts.

"Ummm... Your guess is as good as mine. Whatever it is, she just better hurry up with it. I have things to do, and you have somewhere to be later," I said.

"Yes I do, and I hope she ain't trying to surprise me with no damn toys or teddy bears and stuff like that. I know that I am still young but I'm a little too old for all of that. That lady just better not come out acting all weird or whatever." Layla shook her head.

"Well you wanted to know her and spend some quality time with her so there you go. Whatever she decides to do, you better be ready to bond with her." I laughed.

"It's not funny, but can I ask you a question though?"

"Yeah, shoot!"

"Why won't you give her a chance? I mean, everyone makes

mistakes in life. I know you have. Look at us though, we turned out pretty good despite our upbringing. I don't know. Maybe because I was too young to know about everything that was going on but I don't want to live my life knowing that I could've at least let her try. Just doesn't seem fair that's all."

Layla searched around the parking lot with her eyes, hoping to see Yvette's face but still nothing. Normally, I would brush off anything that was said about Yvette, but what Layla said kind of touched my heart.

She was right. Everyone does make mistakes and I damn sure wasn't perfect myself. Looking at Carter's situation was a perfect example of how a simple mistake can make people think the worst of you.

Carter paid his dues to society in his past life. Now that he has made a lot of changes, it's like everything was still coming back to haunt him and I was a part of it too. It's like God temporarily took someone who I loved the most and exchanged them with someone whose love I needed too. It was just sad that I was too stubborn to accept the signs for what it was.

"It's not that I won't give her a chance, but I can't allow her to enter back into my life as if nothing ever happened. Honestly, I am somewhat over the past but the memories just been coming back. When I look at her, all I can see is the old her. Regardless of what her mouth say on who she changed to be. I can't get passed that and that's a flaw that I am working on. It won't be easy but with time, I'll get better. If she's patient, she will see the results. That's all I have to say about that for now."

"I understand but don't overthink it so much. Like I said, I'm still young and all, but one thing I do know is that I don't have time for all that grown up stuff. Holding grudges, staying bitter, all is just too much. Anyway, speaking of the devil. There she goes." Layla pointed.

Yvette's black Camry finally pulled into the bank parking lot and I flashed my lights hoping she spotted us and she did. She parked next to me and Layla and I got out of the car together. We didn't know what to expect from her but I couldn't sit and wait on her any longer. I had things to do and needed to get them out of the way before I lock myself in my room for the rest of the night.

"Hey girls! Sorry to keep y'all waiting but I had to pick them up." Yvette said.

"Pick who up?" Layla asked.

We were getting impatient and it wasn't hard to tell. Not only did we have to wait on her for almost thirty minutes but now she was referring to the surprise as *them*.

Yvette smiled and tapped the left side window of her back seat. Layla then walked over to me and reached for my hand. For as long as I could remember, whenever Layla felt nervous she would hold my hand. I was always the strong one and the one who protected her. Right now I knew that's exactly what she wanted to feel.

Deep down inside I felt nervous too, but I didn't want to show it. Yvette was still on my shit list so my guards were still up. My gun was under my seat in the car and the only reason why I was feeling queasy inside was because I hopped out of the car without it. Something Carter always trained me to do. He told me to always pay attention to my surroundings, be very attentive, and be no more than inches away from my gun where I could easily pull the trigger whenever I was ready.

Now I was doing the total opposite and praying that I don't regret it. Lord knows that if anything happens to Layla, Yvette could forget that she ever gave birth to us because she would be dead to me after that.

I pulled Layla in close and then two unknown males hopped out of her car at the same time. I was confused as hell, because I didn't recognize any of them and didn't know what the fuck Yvette was up too. Then when they finally walked around the car and stood in front of us with their wide smiles, my heart started racing. I instantly knew who they were, and had to blink a few times to make sure it was real.

"I told you girls that I wanted to make things right. First thing first, I didn't want to keep any secrets away from y'all. You girls deserve more than I ever gave the both of you in life. It wouldn't seem right to keep this away from y'all any longer. I wouldn't be able to live with myself. So, here's my surprise, and I hope we can continue moving forward for the better." Yvette began to cry.

My bottom lip started trembling and my hands were getting sweaty. It almost slipped my mind that I was standing up because there was a point that I couldn't feel my legs either. All of my life I grew up thinking that I was in this world without a father and here he was standing in front of me with joy in his eyes. I looked exactly like him, and there was no way of denying our deep set eyes. From the look of his medium-sized fro, I knew that we also had the same hair texture. Everything about him screamed *me,* and I couldn't believe my eyes after all these years.

I looked over at Layla and she was filled with tears because she felt the same connection as well. We were young girls growing up in the city without a father in sight and that had to be the most hurtful thing that any girl could ever experience in life. Until this day, I would still thank God that we were never raped, drugged, or molested by anyone because of the lack of responsibility on Yvette's end. There had been opportunity after opportunity because of the traffic that she kept going in and out of her house. Now we were standing face to face with the missing piece to our puzzle and I was feeling out of breath but strangely, I felt complete.

"I know that it's a lot to take in and I didn't mean to catch you guys off guard like this. I'm just doing the best that I can and there's no other way than to start off new by doing this here. We've all talked about it and made our peace, now I need for you girls to join in if your hearts allow it. So what y'all say?" Yvette asked.

I instantly tuned her out, and without any control, tears starting rolling down my face. I started to think about all of the lonely days and nights when I needed a father to talk too. The school events, graduations, and the talks about boys that I never had. Before Carter, I knew nothing about men or about life. I was lost and carrying so much baggage at the time. Now that I was older and could see things clearly, I was accepting the fact that all of that pain had really affected me.

Even though I turned out pretty good, I knew I could've been greater. I would've never had to hustle on the block and do things that I didn't want to do. Life had really picked me up and pulled me apart, and it was all because of the father that I thought I didn't have. I hid those emotions for years, but now I couldn't hold it in any longer.

Yvette was too selfish and angry to even care about our well-being back then. Had my father would've been active in my life, all of this would've just been a cordial sit down at a lunch table somewhere. Laughing and talking about life goals with no worries. Just how I always vision it to be.

Regardless of all of the hurt and pain, Yvette had really out did herself on this one and I had to give it to her. If I didn't believe anything that ever came out of her mouth, I believed her today and will continue to do so each day after today.

"Thank you... thank you...." I rushed over to Yvette and hugged her tightly.

"You're welcome baby! This is all I ever wanted. I just wanted to make things right. So, no! Thank you! For allowing me to come back into y'all lives to make things right." Yvette said between sniffles.

I then felt Layla hug me from behind crying along with me.

Before I knew it, we were all in a circle giving each other hugs and wiping the tears off each other faces.

TO MY QUEEN OF COURSE,

How you doing my dark chocolate? My backbone? My everything and more? I hope you're not letting this situation stress you out because you know your man needs you to stay strong until I come back home so we can get back to going hard like we normally do. This is a minor setback! Believe that!

I miss you so much and I just can't wait to sleep in your arms again. I know right now that things may seem confusing because we don't have all the answers that we need but in due time we will. I told my main man which you already know who that I wanted us to just lay low until I figure this all out. I also want you to continue keeping your ears and eyes open for me out there. Sadly, this is not the time for you to cry and vent to anyone you so call trust right now. You have to stay focus! It's us against the world so we have to be on point at all times. Anyway, I don't want to drag this letter out but I just want to keep you in the loop. From what I know and heard so far is that the SNAKE is in our circle somewhere. Not sure on how close or far they are but that mother fucker is near. So keep that game face on and trust that your man got this. Pay attention to your surroundings and keep everyone close to you even closer. Just be ready because when this thing is over and everything comes to the light. I ain't sparing a soul and I won't give a fuck who cries for mercy. I'll get at you when I can and remember that I love you always. Stay focus my queen.

From your husband

I SAT UP IN THE BED WITH MY MOUTH WIDE OPEN. NOT ONLY DID his letter somewhat comfort me but now it has me on edge. We have a snake in our circle and I don't know how he expects me to take all that in. Not once would a thought like that would have come to mind but then again, we were the hood most hated couple. We came from nothing and made something out of it and not too many people wanted to clap for us. Like my husband wrote in the letter though, there's going to be no mercy for the snake once their face is revealed.

YVETTE

"So what do you have for me today? I hope it's something good." I tapped the table with my fingers, anxiously waiting to hear the good or bad news.

We were sitting inside the Denny's restaurant on Biscayne where we always used to meet. I used to always schedule my meetings time with him to be at 8:00 a.m. because I enjoyed having breakfast. Years later and my routine was still the same.

"You know I am good at what I do and I have exactly what you paid me for boss lady." Big- Jay winked.

Big-Jay had been around for years and whenever I needed some PI (private investigation) work done, he had always been the man to call. After he recently found my girl's fathers for me in less than a week, I knew he still had it in him and he never disappoints. It was always strictly business when it came to him and I paid him well too. Big-Jay was always on time and I never had to call him twice to follow up on anything. One request and he got things done expeditiously.

When my old customers wanted to run off without paying me, I would just make one call to Big-Jay and the rest was history. Then when things got real personal with Archie , I had

123

to let Big-Jay take a break for a while until everything cleared up.

I was on so much coke back then that I couldn't even think straight. Whatever Archie said, I did with no questions asked. That day I walked in on him with his belt buckle lose and Kenya was on the floor with tears in her eyes, I wanted to kill him with my bare hands right then and there. Then I thought about how traumatizing that event would've been to my girls and I couldn't put them through that. Even though Kenya thought I failed them as a mother by not taking action first, I couldn't let them experience that. Then when I made them leave, I was only doing what I thought was best. Teddy promised that he would look over them and that was the only reason why I didn't stress myself out too much.

I grew up in a trap house and with both parents running the streets and it changed me. I promised myself that I would never let my kids go through what I did and I failed. I was following in my parent's footsteps and didn't realize it until it was too late. Jumping from foster home to foster home. Then finally running away and going out on my own with no sense of direction in life. My parents were too strung out to even remember me so asking them for help was not an option. Until this day I didn't know where the hell they were. I didn't even care to go looking for them either or putting Big-Jay on payroll to find them. They shitted on me so I shitted on them too.

I also had to thank God for the multiple miscarriages that my mother had after me. I couldn't imagine having a few siblings out there paying the price of those generational curses because I going through it was enough.

Finally the one day that woke up and got my mind together Archie and I drove to Morningside Park one evening where I wanted to have a sit down talk with him. Ten minutes into our conversation and I confronted him about the incident that I walked into between him and Kenya on that day. He looked at me all nonchalant and all his slick ass had to say was that: *She was looking at me like she wanted it.*

My mind instantly went back to my teenage years and I thought about all of the men that I had to fight off growing up. My parents had parties damn near every day and every last person that entered our house was either drunk or high. Not one person cared about the underage child that was in the house witnessing it all especially my parents.

I never wasted my time telling my parents about those incidents because they would've been too high to remember that I told them anyway. One day a friend of my parents repeated the same words that Archie said after I had hit his ass with the lamp that was in my room. It was something that I never forgot and when Archie said the same thing without showing an ounce of responsibility, it triggered something inside of me.

Ain't no way a young girl who knew nothing about men or sex, could have *want it* from a grown ass man. Archie was just like the creep nasty ass men who I grew up around and that's why I didn't give a fuck about sparing his life after. An unexpected rage took over me and just that quick I had a bullet to his head. His body slumped over on the mini bridge that we were standing on, and I smiled as I watched the blood drain from his brain.

I felt so relieved because I finally got revenge for me and my girls. I didn't even bother running out of the park that day because that was something that I would've been proud to sit in prison about. I didn't know how to make up the time that I lost with my girls and saying sorry wouldn't have been enough for them. At least if I had got caught, Kenya and Layla would've known that I loved them unconditionally. They would have known that I wouldn't hesitate to kill for their love and even though I didn't show it how I was supposed to, I know that would've been a start.

Days later and Archie was mentioned on the news once. A

dog walker found his body and that was the end of that. He wasn't shit and no one had even cared to look for him either when he went missing. People who knew him would have said that he deserved it regardless if they knew why he got killed. Archie wasn't living right and everyone who knew him, knew that. Especially the little bit of family that he still had around. I didn't have one bone of care in my body for him because I felt like I was doing him a favor and just basically speeded up his karma for him.

Now I was sitting at the table trying to save my girls again and whatever they thought of me before was going to be history after this if they ever found out.

"Out of all the work I have done for you this has been the most interesting one so far. Little momma has done a lot of dirt in her time, and I don't know how anyone didn't peep who she was already," Big-Jay started off by saying.

"I guess they got blinded. I mean anyone could especially when you don't expect the hate to come from someone you love and took care of." I shrugged.

"We all know that they will be the ones to come at us first."

"Yeah, I suppose."

I had my share of people stealing, lying, and even hurting me in the past. What Big-Jay was spitting out was nothing that I wasn't familiar with. From people I trusted with my personal banking information down to them being around my kids. They all have burned me in a way. That's why I felt nothing for no one except my kids and didn't felt pity for anyone who lived a scheming ass life. At least the dirt I did back then only consisted of me taking those fools money and making them pay me to hold all their shit. Whether it was guns, money, or drugs. They had to cut me a check.

I can proudly say that I never stole from anyone and I don't even owe a mother fucker a dime out there. Not even those crackers. I had no mortgage loans, school loans, car payments, or any credit cards. Everything I ever got in life was paid for in cash and I had always been like that. They only thing I didn't mind paying for now was that damn rent and light bill. Aside from that, I was good from it all.

Kenya and Layla had done real good for themselves. I watched them grow up from afar and was so proud that they never had to sell some ass to get what they needed in life. Teddy made sure of that though. Teddy knew that I was getting on my feet and he promised me that as long as I did, he would do me that favor and keep them safe.

Those girls kept their circle tight and depended on each other for love and support. They never got into any trouble with the law or any drama with girls on the streets. God must have been watching over all of us because he didn't fail my girls at all. Even though they grew up without the love and care they needed from their parents, they were blessed and highly favored.

I know I was too late to expect a change of heart from Kenya and I deserved that. But while Layla is still young and open to having a relationship with me, I wanted to save her before her heart turned cold like Kenya did.

"Anyway let's get back to business. So she was born Marissa Janette Floyd in Albany, Georgia. She grew up with both of her parents until her father started having a drinking problem and became abusive towards her mother. Her father had an injury at work and was later laid off. Due to not having insurance at the time, he never got the therapy that he needed. When the mother couldn't take the beatings anymore, she ran off with her older brother leaving her behind. Marissa was obviously too young for her to keep up with so she took the brother instead. Now with the father being stressed and depressed over everything. It wasn't long until he started abusing and molesting Marissa too. Department of Children and Family later got involved when Marissa had bruises on her arms that her teacher noticed. After too many failed foster homes, at the age of fourteen, she ran off and sadly ended up in the arms of a pimp. She worked for him until she was nineteen and stole every last dime that he had. Knowing that he would be looking for her, she changed her name and got a bus ticket down to Miami where she heard her mother moved too. She tried looking for her mother and had no luck. Since then she had been robbing, stealing, and scheming her way through life. It was the only way she survived. She obviously didn't allow the hurt and pain she endured in life to heal and she's walking around mad at the world. Now she got herself in some mess that she don't know how to get herself out of. So, before it's too late and she runs off again. Here you go. Attached I have pictures, known addresses that she lived at before, and even her mother's contact information if you need it. I hope this all helps." Big-Jay handed me a manila envelope.

I opened the envelope and pulled out the papers and pictures that were inside. I picked up one of Marissa's pictures and couldn't believe how beautiful she had always been. Then I looked at one of her mother's picture and could definitely see the resemblance between the two. I shook my head because all of this could've been avoided if she had just took her daughter with her. It was crazy how sometimes one damn mistake could turn a child's life upside down and I was living proof.

I wasn't there to judge because I made many mistakes of my own but as a mother, I had to do what I had to do to protect mine while I have the opportunity to do so. Even if it meant hurting someone else child who situation had been similar to mine in the past.

"Damn! That's fucked up. This girl is just basically running around with bruises that she never stopped to put a band-aid on. It's like she's angry or wants revenge or something. This shit is very deep but I can't let my emotions get in the way of this though." I tapped the pictures on the table while looking out the window.

"Yeah it's sad and there's a lot of girls like her out here. If I could just share one of their stories, I would be lying. It's unfortunate that it happens to the best of us but what can we do? If the world was perfect a lot of people would be without jobs. Shit, I wouldn't even have a job to do and be able to present this to you too. But it is what it is and the ball is in your court now. Now that you know what you know, you have a move to make. Either you pull back or proceed with your plan." He stared me in my eyes.

Even though Marissa's story was very touching, I couldn't back down now. My girls were drowning and if I didn't help fix their situation soon, they would lose everything that they ever worked hard for. I couldn't do anything about the past but I promised myself that if anything was to ever happen that involves my girls from this day forward. I was going hard for them and wasn't feeling any sympathy for anyone who ever crosses them while I'm still around.

"I have to proceed Big-Jay. Don't get me wrong, I feel sorry for the girl but there's no point of everyone losing because she's hurt. I have to think of mine first because if I don't, I'm not sure if Kenya won't go down for it too. She worked side by side with her husband for years and my heart can't take my babysitting in federal prison. Layla also depends on her so if Kenya gets fucked, it affects Layla too. This shit ain't just about Carter but everyone around him. Including Teddy because I owe him my life. He stepped up to the plate and held my girls down when I couldn't at the time. Not one family member showed up but Teddy did. I don't know what they're doing on their end to get this thing rolling but I'm gonna do my part. So fuck it, game is on!"

"Now that's the spirit. Call me if you need anything else. Just make sure you hold on tight to that information," Big-Jay said.

I stood up from the booth and we exchanged hugs like we always do. Big-Jay was already paid before this meeting because there was no doubt in mind that he wouldn't come through for me. Now my next step is finding out where this girl mother is because if I was coming for Marissa, I had to make sure I keep tabs on everyone she knows. If anything happens to my girls, then she was going to pay big.

KENYA

*A*fter reading my husband's short detailed letter, I woke up feeling reborn again. I was happy that I was able to sleep it off because there was no telling what type of shit I would've been on if I was up and alert. I had so many people on my list who I could've went at directly but I chose to just lay low like Carter advised. When he mentioned that the snake was in my circle that shit crushed my heart, I can't even lie.

What hurt me even more was that we helped, supported, and put so many people on once things immediately picked up for us. I wouldn't know who to point the fingers at right now because our camp was filled with so many successful people. Everyone around us was doing well and getting money just like we were. I couldn't for the life of me think of why anyone would want to set Carter up like that and jeopardize our business. We had put some people in a position to win and that's what was fucking me up right now. Carter didn't owe anybody any money, he had no known beef on the streets, and he kept it one hundred with everyone on his squad. They all knew that he was solid and that's why I know for a fact that it was just a greedy jealous ass mother fucker. I tried my best to wrap my head around it but decided to just let Carter do what he do best.

So with everything that was going on, I had to remind myself to be strong regardless of how heated things were getting. After I dropped Layla off to school, I went ahead and drove down to the city to check on our other investments. This was something we kept away from everyone except for Teddy. Not even Imani knew about them. Teddy was the brains behind it all and Carter and I only trusted his judgment and no one else.

He gave us an opportunity when we were younger even though it wasn't a good one and we ran with it. But with his guidance and mindset, he also gave us a way out. He showed us the way and pierced it in our heads that hustling and fast money wouldn't last forever. Even though Carter and I were young, we knew the value of a dollar because we came from nothing so we valued it even more.

We didn't splurge by buying material things and we didn't brag about how much money we had either. We moved different unlike most of the young folks our age did back then and that's why they hated us so much since the first day. No one knew of any of our moves or what our future plans consisted of. All they knew was that we were hustling on the block for Teddy and that was that.

Later on, after carefully doing our research and finding out what we were interested in and what could bring in some long term revenue, we had a plan and decided to put the hustle somewhat behind us.

Aside from the real estate company, we owned two laundry mats, a car detailing center, and we also franchised a 711. All within a few miles from each other and they were all making numbers.

I know that whoever planted this whole thing thought that they could've destroy us but they couldn't. The only company that was under our names was the real estate one and I kind of regret that. Teddy whose government name and is professionally known as "Garret Dean" had his name sealed on all of our businesses for us. Because we were so young back then, he secured our investments for us and never took a dime away from it.

Even though we have it in writing that all of earnings goes to us, we still preferred to keep him tied to it in case of situations like this. We never thought that someone in our circle would come for us first though. It had always been in the back of my mind that a family member who had never done shit for us would be the first to run us dry but I was wrong.

I spent the next hour running around the city handling business. I made a few local stops, checked on our employees and the cleanliness of our businesses, and last but not least I had a huge bag to take home.

Another smart thing about us was that our safe at home was our bank. We had a few thousands in the bank but nothing that would take our breath away if anything was to happen like it recently did.

As I drove I thought about how good it felt to get out the house to clear my mind. But I knew that it would've felt even better with Carter being next to me.

My phone started ringing in my bag and my hands started shaking. I was hoping that it was my baby because I missed him so much and this was the perfect time to talk to him. I pulled over at a Shells gas station and instantly felt disappointed when a block number appeared on my screen.

I had so much shit going on and wasn't in the mood to deal with anyone playing on my phone right now. I had been receiving blocked calls for two days straight and if it wasn't for Carter being locked up, I would've changed my damn number from the first day.

I sent the call to voicemail and put the car back in drive.

Again, the blocked call was coming in. Frustrated, I slammed my foot on the brakes and put the car in park and answered it.

"Hello!! Why the fuck you keep calling me block? You don't have anything better to do than to play on my damn phone?" I yelled.

"Whoa baby. It's me! Calm down. I definitely need to come back home. I can't have my wife out there stressing like that." I heard Carter's voice say.

"Baby... Oh I'm sorry. I thought it was someone playing on my phone. Why are you calling me blocked?" I asked.

"I"s okay love but I'm using someone's phone. For now on when you see a private number calling you, remember that it's me so answer."

"I'm so sorry. I just miss you so much and wasn't thinking. But any new details?"

"I miss you too love and yes and no. Just know I'm coming home soon. Now listen. I know this might be out of place for you but I need for you to get with Yvette ASAP. She has something for us that will help this situation. Trust me." He assured.

I got silent on the phone because him mentioning my mother took me by surprise. Yvette had been missing in action for years and was just starting to come around. I couldn't for the life of me figure out what she had that we needed from her. Especially with our current situation. Regardless if I understood it or not, Carter was my husband and I know that he wouldn't steer us wrong.

"Yvette huh? Mmmm. Okay! I'm trusting you on this one, baby," I said.

"Believe me. If I could say more, I would. I just need for you to do your part out there and it will all make sense later. Alright?"

"Alright, baby. I love you."

"I love you too. I gotta go but I'll catch up with you later. Don't forget, we can't sleep on this. Call her ASAP!"

"I'm on it baby!"

The call disconnected and I titled my head back on my seat. All of our calls were simply in codes and it was so frustrating trying to figure it all out. But for as long as I known Carter, I knew that he wasn't bullshitting about whatever he knew. He was definitely doing his homework on the inside so I just had to put the pieces together out here with now with the help of Yvette.

I didn't want to waste any more time so I quickly searched Yvette's number in my phone and hit send. Within two rings she answered her phone as if she was waiting on my call.

"Heyyy... How you doing? Umm... I think we need to talk in person." I cut straight to the point with her.

"I'm good and you? And yes we do. What time is good for you because I have a lot of helpful information for y'all."

"You do?" My mouth dropped.

"Yes. Pick a time and place. The clock is ticking." She said.

After setting up of what seem to be a meeting with her, I was left speechless after the call. Whatever Carter and Yvette was up to I knew that it had to be something big. Whatever it was, I was ready for it though.

I used to be so hood and reckless when I had no choice but to be but when I got older and started carrying myself as a professional, I had change a lot of my ways. But for this new found information that I was about to receive. I could tell that I was getting ready to cut some heads off and about my husband and our future, I didn't give a fuck who the victim was going to be.

IMANI

I sat in my car staring at my home while taking deep breaths trying to convince myself to stay calm. I have been in and out of Kenya's place all week doing my best to keep her in high spirits and be a good company to her. By me being a friend though, I also forgot was that Latron's ass still had access to my house. Even though I had my car with me, I'm sure he was still able to get to and from my house with no problem. Not only did I have a broke mother fucker lounging around my shit but I also had someone who I hated with a passion sharing my space with me.

With each passing day, I would find myself waking up and regretting the day that I ever met him. It all started with the first miscarriage that I had and how emotionless he was about it. It was as if I meant nothing to him and I could never understand why he would treat me such way. Especially at a time when I needed him the most.

Then I was foolish enough and allowed myself to get pregnant again, and again he didn't show not one ounce of concern and was even madder that time around. He forced me to have an abortion without asking me how I felt about it and ever since then I created a hate for him that could never go away. The chemistry between us was long and gone. It was as if he was torturing me because he had a team of friends and family members who he could've live with but he chose to occupy his time at my place. It was obvious that he just didn't want anyone to be with me but him.

All I wanted was him gone so I could have my life again. Then hopefully one day Yung and I could go public about our relationship when it's all said and done. Yung was definitely someone who would always love me for me despite my flaws. He would go hard for me just like I would for him. We had the same goals and passion in life. All I had to do now was get rid of Latron but he was currently fucking up all my plans up by just being here.

I exhaled deeply and finally grabbed my things and hopped out of my car. I remembered who I was and had to shake the feeling off. It was *my* house and I wasn't letting no fool run me out of my comfort zone thinking they could get away with doing what they want, when they want.

One thing that I could say that I respected about Carter though was that he was loyal and very giving. He got me my first house as a gift for my birthday one year and paid cash for it too. So even though money wasn't coming in right now and business was on a standstill, I didn't have to work my brain trying to figure out how I was going to pay the mortgage because I didn't have one. Carter blessed me with that house and because of that, I walked around daily feeling guilty inside sometimes.

I honestly can admit that the greed and jealousy had got the best of me but I had took things too far. My thought process was that I wasn't getting any younger, I didn't have any kids, and I eventually was going to need a husband on my arm pretty soon too. With my extended needs list it was only right that I work to have an empire under my belt to match my wants and needs with. Regardless if it meant working hard or scheming for it. I had to get it by any means necessary.

I also had Yung as a perfect candidate so that was perfect. All I needed was the success to go with it and I was happy that he was down to get it with me because it was his time to shine too. He had been a worker for so long and it was time that he owned and ran something of his own.

Carter was family and all but in this day and age, I couldn't think of that or put my feelings on the line because it would do nothing but distract me. This was the risk I was willing to take and I didn't give a fuck how anyone viewed me after it either.

The second I opened the door, I went from 100 to 1000 real quick. I could smell Latron's ass and feet from where I was standing and that only meant one thing. That he been drinking and smoking for days and didn't even bother to take his ass a shower because he was too fucked up to do so. His behavior was only the result of him losing money at the pool hall and that I knew of.

It was the same routine with him and I would always waste time trying to warn him about that place. For one, I didn't want them coming to trash my house looking for him if anything went down like it always did. Latron was arrogant as hell and couldn't take losing and walking out to his car in peace. He always had to start some shit and when he sobers up, I couldn't wait to hear what happened now.

Normally he would call me to come and pick him up but this time, he probably lost big and was too embarrassed to do so. A few months ago, he was almost beaten into a coma because he decided to rob the same people he lost his money to . The human in me prayed for him and lucky for him, my prayers were answered. He covered quickly and it wasn't long until he was back to the same old shit again.

And if it wasn't for Carter and Teddy going out there to make things right with those Potter Boys, Latron would've been dead a long time ago. I hated having anyone in my business and that was another reason why I didn't respect Latron. Word got back to Carter and Teddy and they had decided to handle everything on their own. I begged Carter and Teddy not to mention a word to Kenya because of the embarrassment that I felt. They understood and respected my feelings and did as I asked them. Kenya never mentioned a word to me about the incident with Latron and I didn't open my mouth about it either.

"Let me guess! You lost *all* your money again and now you are going to be laying around here the entire week crying about it huh? But fuck all that, when was the last time you even washed your ass? You have my house smelling like shit and smoke." I slammed the door closed.

I had so much going on in my mind and this was the last thing I needed to deal with once I got home. Kenya and Carter's situation was getting more complicated by the day and without any answers, I didn't know how else to move. Sitting around waiting for things to unfold was affecting my patience and I didn't know how much longer I could wait around.

I started walking around the living room picking up his clothes, shoes, and food plates and cups that he had laying around. I looked over at the kitchen area and that was a mess also. The dishes and the trash can was piled up and I was convinced that something was lying dead in that trash too.

The TV in the living room and bedroom was on and so was every light switch. There was nothing in my house that wasn't out of my place and it did nothing but piss me off even more.

I walked over to the couch where Latron was resting his stink balls on and just as expected, there was a pile of days old vomit stained in front of my couch. He had no respect for himself, me, or where he laid his head at.

I remember how I used to call his family and friends complaining and venting to them about his ways. Then when I realized how worthless he was, I just gave up. They were well aware of what kind of person he was so there was no point of me telling them about something they already knew.

If they didn't care about his health and his life, then why should I? We weren't married or had any kids together. Latron was literally one step away from being homeless and after today, I was changing the locks and moving the hell on with my life.

"Look at you! Just look. You think a woman is going to want you like this? That's why your ass won't leave because you know that nobody will tolerate your shit like I do. At this point, I don't give a damn what you know about me or what you plan to expose either. Matter of fact, I need you to get the fuck out! The truth is going to come out anyway so I don't give a fuck anymore. You can't keep those things over my head any longer." I yelled.

I looked down at him and could hear him laughing lowly with his head face down on the couch. He quickly sat up in the couch and once our eyes locked my stomach instantly turned. He looked so fucked up that I didn't even recognize him anymore. Physically and mentally. He was definitely a whole new person.

He had acne spots planted on his face, he was way overdue for a haircut, and his skin was so dry that it appeared as if he had eczema. I shook my head in disbelief because it was the first time in months that I had actually stopped to carefully look and examine his face and his body. I felt bad for him but then again, I had to remind myself that he wasn't my damn responsibility. Latron was a grown ass man with no worries or responsibility aside from himself. He chose to cater to his bad habits than he did about our relationship. For that reason alone, I had to put out the same energy.

"You done let that nigga dick blow you up in the head. The same way you think another woman won't want me, another man won't want a damn thing to do with you either. You think because Yung is fucking you that you're something special huh?" He laughed.

I blinked my eyelids a few times hoping that I heard him correctly and when the smirk appeared on his face, I knew that I had. Yung was my little secret and we both had worked very hard on keeping our relationship on the low. We had a lot of plans and things that we were working on that was currently in process. Yung wanted the same things that I did and I knew that he wouldn't have leaked out any information about us to anyone. We weren't ready for the world to know about us just yet. Now this fool was sitting in front of me with a smirk on his face as if he had cracked a secret code or something.

"Why you look like you done seen a ghost or something? Let me guess, you thought I didn't know huh? Yung little brother hangs out at the pool hall just as much as I do and the streets talk little momma. So before you talk about all the things that I ain't doing around here, don't forget the mention the hoe activities that you indulge yourself in every day!"

He stood up to his feet and I took a few steps back. The thought of Yung little brother came to mind and he was right. That dude gambled more than anyone that I knew and that's why Yung pulled away from him at times. I was just expecting to come home, shower, and pack some more clothes so that I could get right back to Kenya. With Latron being here drunk and emotional, I just knew that things were going to go left.

"I ain't no hater though but don't you forget who had always been there to help you when no one else will. I was the one running in and out of those banks with you. I was the getaway driver. I was the one taking those long ass road trips. Not that mother fucker you fucking. It was me and you treat me like shit and do what the fuck you want behind my back!" He tried to charge at me instead he tripped over his foot and fell.

I had my back against the wall and for the first time ever, I was scared of him. Mentally, I knew that he wasn't himself. So there was no telling what the fuck was going through his mind especially knowing what he knows about me now. He also was holding in a lot of things from the past but that wasn't anything for him to trip about though. I was there for him just as much as he was for me. He chose to fuck up everything between us, not me.

"You need to get yourself together cause right now, you tripping," I said calmly, trying not to trigger anymore emotions inside him.

"I'm tripping? Naw you tripping. You fucking bitch..." He stood up to his feet and again he came at me.

I didn't have time to run because everything happened so fast. I was now pinned to the wall with both of his hands wrapped tightly around my neck cutting off every circulation in my body. The redness in his eyes had proved to me that he was beyond mad and it was far worse than I ever seen him.

His eyes were locked with mine, and he didn't bother to say a word. Tears were running down my face and I tried fighting him off but I failed with every attempt. My feet were now off the ground and as the room got blurry and my airway was closing in, I knew that death had to be near.

I thought about all the way I cheated in life, stole from people who trusted me, the ones I lied on, and even those I betrayed. This was definitely my karma and if I was supposed to go out this way, then I was ready to meet my maker.

Everything I ever planned to have in life and the goals that I set up for myself was obviously just a dream. No matter how hard I tried, I just could never get ahead in life. I had no kids, no husband, and was obviously going to die that way too.

"You fucking bitch! After everything I've done for you. This is how you do me!" Latron finally released his hold and dropped me on the floor like a piece of trash.

I rolled around in pain trying to catch my breath. I cried like

I never cried before and didn't know what to do next. I didn't know if I should run or lay hopeless on the floor. My throat was burning and everything else ached on my body. It was the kind of pain that I couldn't describe.

"You lucky I didn't..."

Pew! Pew! Pew! Pew!

I heard four shots and Latron body instantly collapsed on the floor right next to me. My heart started racing at the sight of all the blood that was escaping his body and I didn't know what to do because I didn't know where the shots were coming from.

Then when Yung walked up to me, I knew it had to be true love.

"Oh my God baby! I never been so happy to see you. How did you know to come here?" I jumped up and ran into his arms crying hysterically.

"You would normally text or call me once you got home. And when you didn't I got worried. I called you about five times and I didn't get an answer from you. So I said fuck it and did a driveby. I parked a few houses down and got out the car and I scoped out the scene first. When I heard y'all arguing, I decided to just be on standby. Then when I heard it stop, I knew that something was up. Luckily I went with my first mind and didn't leave. Are you okay though?" He caressed my face and looked me in the eyes.

"Yes... Yes... Now I am. I'm so happy you are here. You saved my damn life. If you didn't show up, there's no telling what he could've did to me."

For the first time in life, I felt loved. I felt wanted and it was the best feeling ever. Things weren't perfect between Yung and I but he was perfect for me. Our relationship was unique and the fact that nobody really knew about us made it even more special.

We had time to love and to know each other in peace without the added two cents of other people's opinion about us.

It wasn't how I imagined my relationship would be but it was mine and I embraced every damn thing about it.

"I told you! I will always be there for you. If anyone is fucking with you, they're fucking with me too. I put that on my life. Now what do you want to do about this fool here? We gotta move fast just in case anyone heard those gunshots and decides to call those g's." He asked.

I looked down at Latron's filthy body and almost threw up in my mouth. I was so disgusted with myself and couldn't believe the time and energy that I wasted on his ass. He was holding me back from accomplishing so much of my goals and now he was lying dead in front of me and I didn't feel a thing for him. I didn't shed one tear and I actually felt a load lifting off my shoulders.

I felt so relieved that I didn't have any kids tied to his ass. Then this situation would've been totally different and I probably would've stayed with his worthless ass even longer just because of our damn kids. Come to think about it, that miscarriage and abortion was definitely a blessing in disguise. I wouldn't dare want my kids to be fathered by a man like him. I should've been actually thanking him for forcing me to go to the clinics on those days.

"I know exactly where we can take him and I'll just come back and clean this mess up myself later. For now, let's get suited up and get him quickly the fuck out of here like you said."

I dried my eyes and walked over to the kitchen. Under the sink, I kept a duffle bag with all the equipment that I needed to tightly wrap and seal a dead body. I pulled the bag out and dragged it over to Yung. I dropped it in front of his feet and I smiled at the clueless look that he had on his face.

He bent over and unzipped the bag open. Once his facial expression changed, I knew that he was satisfied by everything that he saw in it. I had everything from saran wrap down to a damn saw in there. I had always been prepared for whatever but

I never thought that I would have to pull out the bag again and use it on someone who I once loved.

"Damn! It look like you've done this before? You are more prepped than me. I can't lie though, it's sexy as fuck though. Anyway, let's get to work." He laughed.

"Well thank you but I can't say that I have though. I am just always ready for whatever. That's all. So let's hurry up and get him out of here." I lied.

I pulled out the two gown sets that I had and handed him one. After my two trips of going to the clinic, I was able to stock up on gowns, gloves, and even a few IV bags. Ten minutes of the nurse leaving me alone in the room and I went on a shopping spree that I obviously benefited from at the end.

Without saying another word, we were now suited up and ready. With gowns, gloves, hairnets, and shoe coverings. All we needed to do was get his body in my car and I had everything else covered.

The blood was nothing to me because after finessing the front desk woman at the abortion clinic back then, I was able to meet up with her for some medication and cleaning supplies for blood. I kept them handy because I knew that another day like this would come.

And Yung was right. I wasn't no professional, but it damn sure wasn't a first for me.

When the only man I trusted ever in my life decided to violate me, I kept his death number in my heart. When I got older and met Latron, his number was finally up. Latron didn't argue or fuss about my reason because he understood why. He rolled up his sleeve and helped me get rid of the body of the man who created me.

Latron's death may have been a sad and tragic one, but it was for the best. He knew something about me that could've put me away for life and I couldn't afford that. All these years of keeping that over my head was finally over. Now I could breathe and live in peace without the paranoia.

I just had to pray that Yung was just as loyal as me because we both couldn't afford to jeopardize our freedom over this.

"I love you, and thank you for always being there for me." I looked at him and said.

"I love you too, baby girl. Trust me, I will always be there for you. No matter what."

TEDDY

"What did she say? Was she okay with it?" I asked.

"Yes she was and everything is good to go. She agreed to meet me at my place at 5pm today." Yvette replied.

"Okay good. Remember, don't lay it out on her too hard. We still have to keep an eye on that girl and with that kind of information it can make anyone do the unexpected. I don't want Kenya going to prison behind all of that. Just put her up on game but don't tell her everything until our plans are in full effect."

"Yeah I know but I can't lie. That shit is hard though. I'm trying so hard not to find this girl and put a bullet in her chest. I spent so many years not protecting my girls and now I finally have the opportunity to do so and I can't." Yvette banged her hand on my desk.

"Trust me. I know how you feel and you will still get that opportunity. We all would want to put one in her but we have bigger plans for her. She ain't no use to us if she's dead. We have to use our brains first because we need Carter out. Once we get a confession out of her, which we will, you can do whatever you want with her after everything is all said and done," I explained.

I was holding my breath and praying that Yvette would get on board with the plan. She was so passionate about her girls and I hate to see her this way. I knew that she changed because I watched her. Those girls meant the world to her and I was just hoping that she didn't fuck our plans up because of her emotions.

We were getting closer and closer and it wouldn't be long until Carter is released and things get back in motion. But first everyone had to be on the same page including Yvette.

"Alright but if this plan don't move fast enough. I'm afraid I'm gonna have to take matters into my own hands. Sorry but I gotta do what I gotta do." She stood up and said.

"Didn't you not just hear one thing I just said? You can't make a fucking move until it's the right time! And I'm not fucking asking you either!" I yelled.

"I don't give a fuck about all that. Why can't we handle this the old school way? I'm not gonna sit around and watch my girls go down for some shit that had nothing to do with him. There's no telling what the damn FEDS are brewing up."

"Ain't shit gonna happen because my uncle is keeping us up to date on everything. So far, everything is looking good. You just have to be patient. What's so hard about that Yvette?"

"Well your cousin better be right because my girl's freedom is at stake here!"

"Fuck you Yvette! She's my daughter too, you know? And did you really use one of my cousins to act like he was her father? You don't think she would know the difference? You went about this all wrong."

The room fell silent and I noticed that her bottom lip was trembling. For years Yvette had kept the truth about Kenya being my daughter away from me. I couldn't believe that she lived on the same block that I hustled out of and I didn't know a thing about Kenya. Even worst, I didn't find out that Kenya was mine until after she started working for me which fucked me up inside even more.

The night that Yvette kicked Kenya and Layla out was the worst and happiest night of my life. Not only did I find out that she was my daughter but she was already introduced to a life that I would've never wanted for her to begin with.

The fact that I hadn't been in her life had also broke my heart and when Yvette asked me to promise her not to mention a word , I didn't know what to do but respect her decision. I couldn't let Kenya know that I was her father after giving her drugs to sell. It wouldn't seem right so I went with Yvette's plan.

And whether she knew I was her father or not, I couldn't let her ruin her life by being on the street with her little sister. So I asked Carter to move her in and everything else was history after that.

By doing that I was able to keep an eye on her as well as her sister. Carter's and Kenya's relationship was out of my control as well but when Carter promised me that he would guard her with his life, I knew that she was safe with him too.

I then had Yvette to give me guardianship rights and I dealt with her from a far after that. She later decided to get cleaned up and turn her life around. Until this day, Kenya still didn't know the truth and that's why I couldn't stay in a room with her for more than thirty minutes. Every time I looked at her I just wanted to sit down and open up to her but I couldn't.

I wasn't no better than Yvette and we both had failed her. I was trying just like Yvette was and I just prayed that the day she finds out, that she forgives us because we were kids raising kids.

"I'm so sorry. I know that she is…. I'm just scared for her. That's all. I didn't mean anything by it. I wanted to tell you and her but I couldn't. I asked him if he didn't mind doing me that favor and he didn't. Once I put a few dollars in his pocket. He was down." She cried.

I walked over to her and wrapped my arms around her. It

was the first time in years that I see her cry and I couldn't help but comfort her. We were both young, dumb, and trying to survive back then. I wished that I was the man back then that I am today. Things would've been totally different for sure. Now we were praying for Carter as well as our baby girl because they needed each other.

"No need to cry sweetie. It will all be over soon. I promise. We just have to stay focus and watch everything fall into place. Do you trust me? Do you believe that I will fix this? And I don't care about him because I know the truth." I lifted her chin and asked.

"Of course I trust you and I'm sorry I got him involved. But I always believed in you because you never once failed me. I trust you with my own life. I just can't believe that I finally have a chance to make things right with them and now all of this is happening."

"I know... I know... We both know that life ain't fair but we can't break down right now. We weren't there for her like we should've been so this time around we have to be. We have to do things right and right now, we gotta save the tears for later. Because at the end, we won't need it. That girl's mother will." I smiled.

Yvette smiled back and I knew that she liked the sound of that. Yvette wasn't nothing to be played with back then. She was always about her money, people respected her, and she had no problem cutting a bitch for crossing her either. I knew that it was killing her inside that she couldn't wrap her hands around that little girl neck and end her. But we had to move a little smarter because this was a delicate situation concerning our girl.

"Okay I'm starting to feel better now." She laughed.

"That's what I'm talking about. Now go out there and meet with *our* daughter and call me later to tell me how it all went." I pulled away and stared at her.

"I will and Teddy. I want to thank you for everything. I mean it. You held it down and the girls grew up to be two beautiful young ladies. I can't thank you enough because if it wasn't for you. God only knows."

"Don't mention it. I only did what a father would and I'm sure if you were in a better position back then, you would've did the same."

She gave me a hug and I watched her leave my house. Yvette would've made a perfect mother and wife but the odds were against us. No one was perfect in my eyes not even me. I never judged her and that's why deep down inside I still loved her. She was my child's mother and if I had the chance to save her too back then, I would. I just wished that she wasn't so stubborn because we all could've been a family by now too.

IMANI

TWO DAYS LATER

"What do we do next?" I turned around and asked Yung.

"You know that whatever you want to do, I'm down to do it too." He caressed my leg.

I was biting down on my nails because I had been a nervous wreck all week. Even though we got rid of the biggest problem which was Latron, his death was coming with so much unexpected heat. The whole time we dated his friends and family didn't show one ounce of concern about him. Now that he's dead, all fingers were being pointed at me because of his so-called disappearance. I was getting nonstop calls, text messages, and even got my car keyed up behind Latron's ass.

Apparently, Latron had told a few of his family members that if anything ever happened to him, that I was to be held responsible regardless of what the news or the streets had to say. I received screenshots from his cousin showing me the text messages between him and Latron on the day he died and my head wouldn't stop pounding ever since.

Hours before I got home, Latron was expressing to him how

much he knew about me and Yung's relationship. How I threatened his life and was treating him like shit. His cousin took those text messages and ran with it. Now his family wouldn't stop harassing me and it was eating me up inside. Just when I thought I was in the clear, this shit was getting so deep that I didn't know how much I could take anymore.

I wanted to call Kenya for help but she had enough going on to even care about me right now. I had no other friends or family members to reach out to so I was fucked. All I had was my man on my side and I was just hoping he was down with this new plan of mine. My plans were not going as planned and since it wasn't. I didn't see the point of us living in this damn city any longer. I was creating enemies by the day and could see how things were going to turn out already if we didn't leave any time soon.

"What are you thinking about?" He asked.

"Why don't we just pack our bags and get a fresh start somewhere else? You know, a change in scenery?" I questioned.

"Where is all of this coming from? I thought we were going to open all of our business here. Miami is a busy city, where are we going to get more foot traffic than here? Where Imani?" He sat up and asked.

Yung had a point but he wasn't seeing the bigger picture. Once everything comes to the light about Carter and especially about Latron's death, there wouldn't be a business for us to open and run. Even though he helped me get rid of Latron's body, I didn't tell him about the threatening phone calls and messages that I've been receiving. I was scared of shit and still sleeping in my home which made my anxiety even worse. I tried to get us a room for the week but he refused because he hated the hotel bedsheets and towels. I was hoping that the hot sex that I gave him earlier would convince him but it didn't seem like he was going to budge either.

"I know Miami is booming with people and tourists every day but maybe we just need to venture out elsewhere. It's very competitive here and there's no telling if our business ideas are gonna be a success once it's all put into place."

"Every business takes time to take off. You just have to believe in yourself and put in work. Then watch it work itself out. Honestly, what's really bothering you? This doesn't sound like you." He stared at me.

Tears started to roll down my face because he was the only person I cared about and I was putting his life at risk for me. All my life I had been a fuck up and the one time that I finally found someone who I didn't have to share or fight for and this happens. It wasn't fair to Yung at all because he was just doing every damn thing wrong because of me. He didn't have any kids or had he been married before. Here I was making him my Clyde and I wasn't even worth it.

I unlocked my phone and opened the text message that I received from Latron's cousin and showed it to him. I watched as he read through the messages and could see the veins popping up on the side of his head. Tears kept rolling down my face because I knew that it was the end for us. I knew that after he read those messages, that he would up and leave me without a doubt. Just like everyone else in my life did so I wouldn't be surprised if he did the same.

"Why the fuck didn't you tell me about this sooner Imani? This is dangerous and we been here just chilling at the crib like nothing is going on. Are you even thinking straight? Is that why you want to leave Miami all of a sudden?" He snapped.

"I'm sorry! I'm so sorry. I didn't know how to tell you and didn't want you to leave me because of it. I didn't think that Latron's death would bring so much attention. Those people never gave a damn about him especially when he was out drunk and gambling every damn day. They always told me to deal with it. I didn't know what to do. I'm sorry, baby... I didn't know." I cried.

"This ain't nothing to play around with Imani. Get your things and let's get the fuck out of here. There's no telling what his cousin has planned for us. I wish you had said something to me sooner. I don't even have my damn gun with me. Fuck!"

I jumped up out of the bed and did exactly what I was told. I didn't bother packing any clothes. Instead, I grabbed my purse, my keys, the money from my safe, and my phone charger. I left everything else because I knew that I could replace them wherever we ended up at. I hated that he had to find out this way but I didn't know what else to do. If I could turn back the hands of time, I would. I'm just happy that he is handling it better than expected.

"Let's go!" He yelled. He was done throwing on his clothes and shoes then he roughly grabbed my arm. I almost bumped into the bedroom wall while running out but I was quick enough to dodge it. The second we stepped outside I took in the fresh air and smiled. For some strange reason, it calmed me instantly. It was as if I wouldn't have the opportunity to smell it again so I was taking it in slowly.

"Let me guess? This was because of them too?" He pointed at my car that was keyed all over.

I saw it this morning when I woke up and I walked right back in without telling him a word. I was hoping that he wouldn't leave the house all day and not notice it. Or by the time he left, it would be night fall, and it would definitely be too dark for him to see it.

"Yes. I believe so." I looked at him with puppy eyes.

"Don't worry. We gonna be okay. Just get in the car and drive. We will figure this all out in a little bit. First, we have to get out of here safely." I pressed the unlock button on my key and he opened the driver side door for me.

I did as he said and quickly jumped in without saying

another word hoping not to piss him off even more. I started the car and placed the car in reverse but instantly slammed on my breaks when I looked in my rearview and saw the unexpected.

"What the fuck? Who fucking car is that?" I looked back and noticed that I was blocked in by a car that I didn't recognize.

"Do you know who that is?" Yung asked.

"No. Do you? They pulled up like they know us or some shit."

"Hell no! Fuck! I can't believe I'm not strapped. Any other day I'm on point with my gun on my side but out of all days, I'm slipping. This has got to be some shit." He snapped.

Yung banged on the dashboard and I could see it in his eyes that he was frustrated as hell with me. Not only did I keep those messages away from him but I had him chilling at my house all comfortable and all.

He always kept his gun on him no matter what but I told him that when he's with me that he should feel safe. Even though he hesitated a little, he eventually ended up leaving his gun at home and decided to spend a few days with me without it. Now I was regretting that I made him do that.

"Get the fuck out the car bitch!" Yvette opened the door and yelled with a gun pointing at me.

I knew that I was going to have my run in with that bitch one day but I didn't expect for it to be like this. Yvette spent years neglecting her daughters and now she wanted to come back into their life like everything was alright. She noticed that I could see right through her phony ways and that's why she instantly had a problem with me from the first day she met me.

"What the fuck do you want Yvette? I suggest you mind your damn business and leave when you can." Yung threatened her.

"Don't play stupid! And when it comes to my girls, they're *my* business! Y'all made this shit personal so get y'all asses out the car now and I'm not going to say it twice." She yelled.

I turned to look at Yung hoping he would give an answer but before I could open my mouth to warn him about the man standing on the opposite side of the door. The passenger side door swung open and Yung was hit behind the head with the end of the man's gun. And when I turned around to face Yvette, so was I.

YVETTE

"$\mathcal{G}$et y'all asses out the car. I'm done playing these fucking games with y'all. If y'all ain't heard about me, now you have. And bitch you was way over due for this ass whooping anyway." I yelled.

I watched as Joey and two of my young hittas, Kilo and Monti, pulled Imani and Yung out the trunk of the car. I remembered the look that they had in their eyes when they saw me walk up to the car, and the shit was priceless.

They didn't see me coming and I loved it. After everything that is going around the city about them, I knew that they were expecting Latron's team and not me.

When word got out that Latron's cousin had a hit on them, I knew I had to move fast. If I hadn't showed up to her house when I did, those fools was going to be long gone on I75 some-where. It was a good thing that I was thinking with my brain than anything else.

I know that Teddy wanted me to take my time with this but I couldn't. Once they would've got in that car, there was going to be no word or sight of them ever again. Their life in Miami was over with. Not only were they in deep waters about Kenya and

Carter but they also had Latron's friends and family to worry about.

"Dawg I'm sorry but you know I gotta do what I gotta do." I heard Joey say to Yung.

They had been Teddy's number one hittas aside from Carter and I knew that bringing Joey along would cut Yung so deep that he would be begging to be set free. Joey and Yung had been tight forever and everyone knew it. Then when I offered Joey a nice check, he was down for the ride regardless of their friendship.

I knew that Yung seeing Joey would bring back a lot of memories and I wanted to fuck with him as much as I can.

The two exchanged mean looks and Yung and Imani where escorted into the run down trap that Teddy owned in Liberty City.

The grass looked like it hadn't been cut in months, the paint on the house was chipping off, and from the sewer smell that I picked up when I walked through the yard. I knew that the septic tank was full. Regardless of the terrible landscape and up keeping of the place. That trap made money.

Everyone knew where the trap was located at but most importantly, they knew not to fuck with any of Teddy's investments either.

"What the fuck Yvette?" Teddy jumped up from the table and said.

I looked around the room and it was empty just how I liked it. But on the table that was centered in the living room, Teddy had his guns and drugs stretched out on it which was very visible. Even though Teddy had retired from the streets and went legit. He didn't mind showing the other dudes from the hood on how to get money and secure it. Teaching was his passion and I wasn't surprise by the role he was playing in some of those young boys life.

"Listen, if I didn't pull up on them when I did those mother fuckers was going to be long and gone by now. Then what? I caught them sitting in her driveway getting ready to take off." I explained.

The boys tossed them on the floor and I could hear Imani crying on the floor already. She was so wicked and spent her life fucking people over. I couldn't believe that she was actually in here crying real tears and shit.

If she thought she was crying, she didn't see a damn thing yet.

"Oh is that right? So you were just going to turn your back on your friends and leave them just like that huh? After everything they have done for you? I knew Carter should've cut you off when he had the chance but he couldn't get over the fact that you guys were family. You would've had me fucked up! Family or not, I know a snake when I see one," Teddy walked over and said.

I stood at the doorway with my arms crossed before my chest waiting on Kenya's arrival. The second I had Imani and her dude inside the trunk, I texted Kenya the new location that I wanted to meet her at.

Originally we were supposed to meet up at my house so that I could show her everything that Big-Jay had given me but this was much bigger than any paperwork ever. I wanted Kenya to be able to look her fake ass friend in the eyes while Imani confess everything she had ever done to Kenya and her husband.

True, I wasn't the perfect mother, daughter, or maybe even girlfriend. But I damn sure was never a snitch and I never envied anyone for what they had either. I always worked hard or hustled for what I wanted in life. I never had to ruin another woman's life to get what I needed and Imani violated every friendship rule in the book. She did beyond the belief and now karma had finally pulled her number so today was her day.

Yung and Imani were now on their knees with their hands

still tied behind their backs. I was smiling to myself because for once I had done something good for my girls. It wasn't much but it damn sure was a start.

If I had did everything that I was supposed to in order to protect my girls back then, they wouldn't be in this situation. Even though I can't change the past and it's too late to do so. I was finally able to do something right and now this time around I was going to make sure that another mother fucker never get the opportunity to hurt my girls again. And I don't give a fuck how old they are.

"You know what? Fuck all y'all! I'm gonna die anyway so I'm not gonna spend my last few minutes here on earth begging for my life. Y'all can have that. And yes, I did betray my damn friend. Who hadn't? So everyone got on top by being loyal? Yung and I was just trying to make it out and make a name for ourselves. We spent years working, playing taxi, security, and being a runner for everyone here. When was it going to be our turn? We want to sit back and make orders too. We want to wake up and see commas in our account too. So, if I had to cross a few close love ones to do so, then fuck it. I guess I'm guilty then," Imani said.

I looked at the reaction on everyone's face and there was not one look of concern on it. They didn't give a fuck what she was talking about just like I didn't and she was right, she was going to die anyway so why care?

"But had I known that's how you felt then we could've went harder on your dreams also? You didn't have to burn me, jeopardize our business, and ruin my husband. I haven't seen him in months and all your selfish ass was gonna do was run off and leave him in there? That's your cousin Imani? Does that mean anything to you?" Kenya said once she walked in.

Imani lowered her head to ashamed to even look back at Kenya. She knew what Kenya was saying was nothing but facts. I've watched Kenya take on the responsibility of being a sister and mother to Layla when I was too fucked up to be a parent to them. Kenya was loyal, loving, and cared about everyone she came in contact with. The way I watched her care for Layla, I knew that she would grow up to be a decent human being. And if Imani knew her how I did, she knew that Kenya was being sincere about what she said.

"Her brother... Carter is her brother," I said.

"What!" Kenya yelled.

I pulled the paperwork out of my pocket and handed it to her. Now the facial expression of everyone in her room had changed including Yung.

"Carter was your brother the whole time?" Yung asked Imani.

Imani still had her head bowed and didn't bother to make any eye contact with anyone in the room.

"She don't have to answer that question because I will. Yes, Carter is her brother. Her big brother at that. And her name is not Imani. It's Marissa. After her mother left her with her father, who later molested and raped her, they moved to Miami and technically forgot about Imani. I'm sorry, Marissa. She grew so much hate over the years for them that she later killed her father and framed her brother. The jealously grew so strong for her brother that she wanted to destroy him in any way that she could. Now she's here on her knees about to take her last breath before all of us." I smirked.

The room fell silent but no one was angrier than Teddy. I knew that his emotions was getting the best of him because for years he allowed Imani to be around because of Carter. She had access to their financial accounts, statements, and she even used to lock up the office and make the bank deposits for them on certain days.

Imani knew how to do a lot of shit in which could put Carter away for life. Carter was a good dude and from what I heard, he was alright with me. Imani's greed fucked everything up for her and now she was just a dead woman walking.

"Bitch I should blow your fucking brains out!" Joey pointed his gun behind Imani's head.

"No... no... As much as I would love for you to end this bitch and dump her ass off somewhere, we can't. We need a confession on paper because we gotta get Carter out. He been in way too long and right now, she's not even worth us cleaning up after. Her or her shady ass nigga," Teddy said.

Yung now had his head lowered as well and Imani's cry was getting louder and louder.

I looked over at Kenya and she had the most disappointing look on her face. As much joy as it brought to my heart to expose her friend, I was hurting now because my daughter was. No one really wants to hear some shit like that about a close friend especially one who you would give your last too.

I walked closer to her and gently wrapped my arms around her. For the second time, Kenya then laid her head on my shoulder and it instantly warmed my heart. She didn't deserve none of this and that's why I wanted to make sure that after today, I go hard by keeping her and her sister safe.

"Get this bitch some paper and one of y'all pull out a phone. We need this shit on paper and on recorder. She gonna say everything and she better not miss one word," Teddy said.

"How we gonna know she telling the truth?" Joey asked.

"If Carter comes out then we know. If not, she might as well get ready to share a casket with her little boyfriend over there."

"Sounds good to me."

When I saw the tears running down Kenya's face I decided that it was best that she left the trap. It was obvious that her friendship with Imani had completely ended and she heard everything that she needed too. Right now, I just had to make sure that she stayed focus and didn't stress herself out until things were finalized until we get her husband out.

"Listen, I'm sorry that you had to find out this way but I had to do what I had too. I was never a mother to you girls and I felt like I had to do something to protect y'all for once. I know this was not something that you wanted to know about her and honestly if it was me, I would be fucked up inside too. I just hope you don't take this personal or hold anything against me. I was only trying to help and with the help of Teddy of course, we got down to the bottom of this. Despite of what he originally had planned for us to do. I just couldn't sit back and watch that damn girl get away with this. Over my dead body." I expressed.

At first I was numb to the whole situation but when I saw all the emotion in Kenya's eyes, I had no choice but to picture me being in her shoes. She was still young and learning about things in life even though she think she knew most of it. One thing she had to experience was the betrayal of friends because me being a family member, had already accomplished that.

I really wished that Imani was loyal and solid like Kenya was to her but life wasn't perfect. And when it came to a woman like Kenya who had a good head on her shoulders and a drive to kill for, she needed to be aware that she will always be a target. Friends or not, someone will always want what she wants. It's just sad that it was someone she trusted and loved like a sister.

"Honestly those tears that I just shed was tears of relief. For months I had been fighting with myself. Trying to put the pieces together and I always ended up at a dead end. With Carter saying so much in so little words, I just couldn't wrap my head around it. I knew there was a snake in the circle but Imani was definitely the last one on my list. You have to understand. She had been around since... you know. Since Carter and I got together and she had never left our side since. We would've never thought it could've been her. Whatever I had, she had. And when anybody saw me, they saw her. This is so unreal." Kenya dried her face.

There was a silence between us and we both were in deep

thoughts about the situation. I had to agree with her. It was a lot to take him but I rather she found out now than later.

"I know it is but we can't dwell on that. She made the decision to go against you and now she has to deal with the consequences. In the meantime, let's try to figure out how we're going to expedite your husband's release." I caressed her back.

"I know that you didn't have to do what you did but I thank you. I really appreciate you and I don't know how I could ever repay you," she looked at me and said.

"You never have to repay me because you're my daughter. I'm happy that I made those changes because there's nothing that I won't do for you and your sister. I prayed for days like this and my prayers have finally been answered. You girls won't be disappointed. I love y'all."

"Thank you! I love you too mom."

CARTER

I was finally a free man and there was no greater feeling that being home with the people who really loved me. I didn't know how to thank Teddy enough for holding things down and staying on top of things. Whenever I called him, he answered and laced me up on everything that was going on.

When Yvette's private investigator got in contact with me, I couldn't believe my ears. But nothing about my momma surprised me. She kept so many secrets away from me and Giovanni that there was no telling what that lady had up her sleeves.

Then I quickly got in contact with Teddy and we just sat back and watched everything play itself out.

Once the Feds got a hold of all the evidence and the confession from Imani, it felt like a weight was immediately lifted off my shoulders. Imani had tried to ruin me and what my wife and I had built together but she didn't go hard enough. Now her greed had her sitting in a federal cell feeling the same pain that I felt for months.

"Are you okay baby? You haven't said anything?" Kenya asked.

"Of course. I'm just taking all this in and enjoying the moment. That's all," I said.

Kenya had planned a family dinner my first week out and just seeing everyone I love including Yvette's face, brought nothing but happiness to my heart. Everyone didn't have to come together for me the way they did but they went all out.

"I gotta give it to you Carter. If I was in your shoes, I would've killed that damn girl. Family or not," Yvette said.

"Believe me. I was fucked up in the head about it just like everyone else. But I couldn't bring myself to kill my own sister. Regardless of how I found out, she was still my sister at the end. I just know that if she didn't go through the things that she did in life, she would be sitting here with us today. That girl was just walking around with a lot of bruises that she didn't allow herself to heal. In situations like that, eventually someone was gonna get hurt by that girl. Sadly, I was one of her victims."

"You know what? That's some real ass shit you just said. That girl really was just trying to survive like we once were. I just wish that things had turned out differently for her because she hurt a lot of people in the process. Damn, that's crazy. It really happens to the best of us." Yvette picked up her drink and took a few sips of it.

"I agree but as you can see, she wasn't raised on love. Just survival. Imani knew exactly what I went through in life as well. It's not like our backgrounds didn't compare. It's just sad that she went about it all the wrong way. If she would've at least gave a sign or something. I would've reached out and helped her. I just wished I knew that something was wrong. I wish I knew that she was reaching out for love and attention." I banged my hand on the table.

The sound of my hand hitting the table startled everyone including myself. I didn't know how personal I took the situation until now. I spent months praying and working hard on getting out. Now that I was, I was feeling fucked up inside.

Imani spent most of her days and nights with me and I never picked up on at least one sign that something was wrong. Not only did my life get put on hold because of her wrong doings, now she was in jail battling her own demons as well.

To everyone it might've been what she deserved but I was never the type to judge anyone. We all had a background and neither one of us who was sitting at the table was better than her.

"Baby, I can completely understand how you feel about the situation but I don't want you to beat yourself up about it. None of us do. Right now let's just enjoy this dinner and we'll figure out the rest later. It's your first week out and Imani is where she needs to be for now. Remember, it could've been you still sitting in that jail cell hoping on a miracle to happen," Kenya said.

Even though I somewhat agreed with what she said, I just nodded my head to end the conversation. I knew that Imani being in there wasn't going to sit right with me. Especially knowing now that she was my sister and not my cousin the whole time. I definitely have to reach out to her to at least make peace with her. I didn't want her feeling like she was alone because she had been for so long. And in result of that, things had lead down to this.

"Also I wanted to say something," Kenya stood up and said.

We all looked around the table patiently waiting on whatever it was that she had to announce. We had been through so much for so long and I just wished that this family finally got some good news for once.

"Is everything okay baby?" I caressed her hand.

"Yes it is. I just wanted to express this so we all could stop with hiding secrets around here," she said.

"What do you mean?" I sat up straight in my chair.

"For one, Teddy I have to say that I respect you. I respected you since day one. From the day that you took me and my sister in. Until this day, you are still around and keeping it real with our family. When my mother introduced me to my so call father, I knew something wasn't right. Aside from the excitement I felt when she told me, I felt nothing. But when I went home and thought about it, I was finally able to put things together. After doing my research and also hiring my own private investigator, I found out that *you* were really my father. That news did nothing but bring happiness to my heart as well as disappointment. You were closer than I thought and I was happy that you never left our side. I say that to say this, I thank you. I'm not mad but I just wanted you to know what I already know that you knew. There's no hard feelings or anything and I appreciate you for doing what you did. There's not too many men around here like you left and I thank God that you kept me and Layla save all of these years."

The room was silent and I was speechless. For the first time Teddy looked emotional and I never had seen him like this. He was in deep thoughts and obviously searching for the words to say. We all exchanged looks back and forth from each other because I knew that we were all thinking the same thing.

"Baby girl I always wanted to tell you but with the agreement I had with your mother, we just decided not to. We were all young and was parenting all wrong but we did our best. Really we did. I just hope that this doesn't change anything about us because if I could go back and change some things I would." Teddy expressed.

"Honestly, I am fine. I just wanted to break the ice so there wouldn't be any awkwardness between us. I am just happy that we are all here together and having this meal like a real family should.

"Please forgive me baby. We were just..."

"It's okay. There's no hard feelings and I forgave you guys since the first day. I'm too blessed in life to hold grudges. This is a fresh new start for us all so let's continue to move forward," Kenya said.

'Well I guess we can all toast to that."

∾

AFTER YESTERDAY'S DINNER AND THE FEELINGS THAT WERE expressed, I spent all night thinking about everything in life. My past, my present lifestyle, and even more. My mother.

When I saw her walking the street awhile back, visions of her had took me back to Imani's situation. They were both looking for love and someone to save them and because they didn't have anyone, they allowed life to get the best of them.

I promised myself that I wouldn't let another soul in my circle go through anything that Imani had to go through. I didn't have the chance to save Imani but I definitely have the opportunity now to save my mother.

This was something I needed to do for myself and my mother because I had to been carrying around hate in my heart which I allowed to live for too long.

I was sitting at the Walgreens parking lot on 54 Street waiting to see her walk by. After making a few phone calls, I got word that this was her hustling spot on most days. I was told that she would walk up and down this strip begging drivers and pedestrians for change and that made me feel some kind of way. I was also told that her mental health was at risk too. My sources told me that she could be found talking, yelling, and even crying to herself at times.

When I got all the information that I needed, I quickly disconnected the call. I couldn't stand to hear another word and now all that was left for me to do was save her from the streets before things got worse.

After waiting for ten minutes and not seeing her, I hopped out of the car and decided to walk and stand under the street light. Hoping to catch a better view of any sight of her. It was just my luck that the minute I got there, she was waiting to cross the street that was adjacent from me.

She had on the same black and brown dirty ripped up clothes that I saw her wearing the last time I was sitting in the car with Teddy. Her hair was still matted and the shoes she had on was ruined as well. From the way the clothes were hanging off her, I could tell that she had drastically lost a lot of weight too. My heart was aching for her and I felt ashamed that I was her son and she was living like that.

Here I was living and sleeping comfortable in my big ass house with only Kenya inside and my mother was out in the streets trying to survive this thing call life.

I took a deep breath and didn't bother to wait for her to cross the street so I walked over to approach her. With each step that I took, I just prayed that she didn't run off on me because she was afraid. I wasn't sure if she was on drugs or anything because I knew the effects of that. The irrational behaviors, violent tempers, and being combative when approached at times. Aside from when I used to sell drugs in my younger days, I used to watch the crack heads go at it all the time.

I was finally face to face with her and once she saw me standing in front of her, she looked up at me and I could see the gloss in her eyes.

"Hey, how you doing? Do you need help crossing the street?" I touched her gently on her left arm in hopes of her not panicking and running off.

"My son! Of course I do." She smiled.

My hand began to tremble and I was feeling weak in the knees as well. The temperature was at least 95 degrees outside so the heat wasn't making it any better for me to focus. The sound of her saying *son* brought so many emotions over me that I didn't know what to do next.

I wasn't expecting for her to recognize me but here I was faced and reunited again with my mother.

"Damn! You remember me?" I asked.

"Of course I do. I see you all the time just as much as you see me too. I had been waiting for this moment for a very long time. I missed you, son," she said.

Tears started running down both of our faces because deep down inside we had both needed each other and it showed.

For the next twenty minutes, we drove in the car talking and catching up on life. I had bought her some food to eat and watching her swallow every bite broke me inside. I knew that it had been a long time since she had a hot meal, but I promised her that after today, she would never miss a good meal ever again.

"Just so you know, I'm not on drugs or anything. I'm no trick either. I ain't doing none of that. I know people see me on the streets and instantly make those assumptions about me. I don't blame them though. Shit, look at me. I would think the same thing to if I was them." She laughed.

"Honestly I didn't assume anything. I mean, I heard a few things but I didn't take off with it. I wanted to see and talk to you myself," I expressed.

"Yes son. There's nothing for you to explain because you came out of me. You have always been that way and I fucked up when I didn't embrace you the way that I should have. The one who I spoiled rotten didn't even love me back. If it wasn't for the clothes and shoes that I bought him, he wouldn't have gave a damn thing about me. But you? You were always the responsible and dependable one. I honestly don't know where I went wrong." She looked out the window.

Memories of me growing up in the house with her and Giovanni was slowly coming back. I could remember always being the cook, the maid, and handyman while Giovanni enjoyed his teenage years like every teenager should have. I didn't regret it though because I turned out to be a damn good husband, friend, and business partner to everyone around me. I just wished that our childhood was a little better though.

"Whatever happened to him? You know Giovanni... Sergio... Have you heard from them?" After the questions came out of my mouth, I had regretted even asking.

"Honestly, I don't even know. Giovanni went and lived his life, and you know Sergio had a family the whole time. I was just someone he came to when things wasn't right at home. Giovanni just happened to be our karma for messing around. That's all," she confessed.

I nodded my head and stayed focused on the road. When I was younger I didn't understand what was going on but of course it all made sense now. My father was long and gone and Sergio came and left when he felt like it. All I thought was that he was traveling or working or something because of his business attire that he always had on. Now it all made sense and I respected her for being honest about it.

"Where have you been living? How do you survive out there and stuff?" I was so curious that I couldn't even help but ask so many questions.

"There's an abandon house that I stay at, and the neighbors next to it feed me and allow me to shower in their backyard at times. These rags that I am wearing is just something to throw people off. If I went around asking for money in clean clothes and talking proper,you really think someone would help me? Naw! Even mother fuckers I grew up with won't stop to help me but it's alright though. I've been surviving out here on my own. I'm basically paying for everything that I have done in life. Sleeping with a married man, kicking you out the house at such a young age, and treating you like shit."

"Also leaving behind your daughter Marissa," I added.

The smile and smirk that she had on her face instantly changed to a frown when I mentioned my sister's name. I knew that it was personal to her because she not once ever mentioned us having a sister growing up. We played together with Imani the whole time and come to find out she was our sister not my cousin.

"Marissa... Marissa... oh my poor baby. That girl endured so much pain. I should've never left her with that nasty ass bastard. I was so young Carter and I didn't know what to do. Her father went from being a good family man to beating me to the point that I couldn't even wake up on some days. When I finally had the opportunity to escape, I just left. Marissa was sleep at home and you and me were already out at the grocery store together. I knew that if I had went back to get her with him being at the house, that I wouldn't have the opportunity to make it out. I wasn't thinking straight and with the money that I had on me, I got us a bus ticket and just left." She cried.

"Why didn't you go back for her? Why? That girl is ruined now and there's nothing we can do to change that." I banged on the steering wheel.

I quickly pulled into a Walmart shopping plaza because I was too emotional to drive. Imani could've had a chance in life if all our mother had to do was take her with us or go back to get her. I could never imagine leaving a child behind. I would kill myself first before I do but again, I wasn't in her shoes.

"I wanted to, Carter! I really did. That man was the devil, and if I had went back there was no telling what he could've did. He was so evil and angry and most likely he would've been liable to kill us all. We probably wouldn't have been here today talking if I did. Trust me, that is something I beat myself up about all the time. Marissa also used to drive around and torture me to because she hated me that much. She eventually found me later on, expressed to me how she felt, and every time she sees me she reminds me of what I did. I've been living with all this shit my whole life. I have nothing Carter. No husband, not my kids, I don't even have my life. I fucked up. I know all of this. Believe me" She continued crying.

Ignoring the filthy clothes and odor that stained her body, I leaned over to hug her tightly. I had missed her so much so at this point I didn't give a fuck what she had done in the past. I needed my mother back and I didn't want to go another day without making things right between us again.

We all made mistakes in life, and I wanted to at least make one of mine right. I could've did the same thing to and turn my back on her but this was my calling. I had to make things right with everyone. It was something about those jail cells that makes a person reflect on things and I definitely came out a brand new man.

"I'm sorry for asking those questions. I really don't give a fuck about all of those things. I just want to make things better between us that's if you want to. I spent my whole life without you and even though I am married now, I still lack the love and affection from a mother. I can admit." I pulled back and looked in her eyes.

"Do you have any kids yet? Please don't tell me that I missed out on watching my grand babies grow up." She smiled.

"No not yet but now that my family is almost complete, Kenya and I can for sure start working on them now." I smiled.

After a few moments of pouring our hearts out and talking about everything that we could ever think of. We were now pulling into the driveway of my house and I could see the smile widening up on her face.

I was happy to bring her home with me because now she would never have to worry about someone else feeding her or taking any cold showers in someone's backyard.

She was going to have full access to her own room, bathroom, refrigerator in her room, and a nice comfy queen size bed. She had always been the number one lady in my life even though I didn't know it as a child. Now I was going to treat her like the queen that she always was regardless of how she treated me back then.

"Are you ready to go inside and meet my family?" I asked.

"Of course I am. Your house is so beautiful son. You did well for yourself. I am so proud of you baby."

"It's *our* house. Welcome home momma. This time around I am never letting you go. I promise."

I saw the excitement in her eyes and it made me feel soft inside. I knew that once she got to know everyone that she would never want to leave also. Kenya was easy going, loving, and would do anything for anyone she cared about. So I knew that once I brought my momma home, that she would welcome her with open arms like I did.

We hoped out of the car and started walking towards the house. The second I unlocked the door the smell of Kenya's cooking instantly invaded our nostrils and we were pleased. Momma titled her head back and closed her eyes and I knew that it warmed her heart to smell a home cook meal again.

"Baby, is that you?" Kenya walked up to me and said.

"Yes it's me, baby. I want you to meet someone."

Momma nervously walked up from behind me and exposed her face. I wrapped my arm around her giving her the assurance that she was safe and welcomed into our home too.

"Kenya, I would like for you to meet my mother," I said.

The smile on Kenya's face was everything to me because for years she heard my story and always pushed me to look for my mother. Now we were here in the flesh and I knew that inside she felt proud of me.

"Nice to meet you and welcome to our home. Come on and let me get you settled in," Kenya said.

I nodded my head to let her know that she was safe and without any hesitation, momma followed behind Kenya and I knew that was going to be the start of something great.

❧

AFTER GETTING MOMMA SETTLED IN I DECIDED TO SPEND THE
night writing a letter to Imani. She was next on my list and I
didn't want to go to bed without expressing to her how I feel
and also letting her know that I forgive her for everything that
transpired between us.

HEY SIS,

*I HOPE THAT THIS LETTER BRINGS YOU NOTHING BUT COMFORT
because I know that writing this have done the same for me. I found
our mother the other day and she had been doing and looking better
since the first day that she made it here. The situation between you
and I had truly been an eye opener for me and honestly, I can't fault
you for your actions. You were young, lonely, confused, and just trying
to find your way in life. I just wished that you had reached out to me
like you should've have and we all could've been in this house celebrating our mother together. Please be aware that this letter is not
meant to come down on you but to just say that I understand and I
accept your apology. If I was in your shoes, I probably would've did the
same thing to. Life is hard sis and I am sorry about all of the things
that you had to experience on your own out there. But I just want you
to know that you will not do this time on your own because I will be
there for you every step of the way. I'm sorry that it had to go down
the way that it did but that was real of you. You know to take responsibility of your actions and all. That takes guts and I respect that.
Come to think about it, you remind me of myself so I guess we really
are related. (I hope that made you smile). Again, I hope that things can
get better between us because at the end of the day we are all family. I
love you and I can't wait to hear from you soon. Stay up sis, it will all
be over soon. Trust me.*

Love big bra

ONCE I ENDED THE LETTER AND SEALED THE ENVELOPE, A TEAR drop fell on top of it. Today had been such an emotional day for me and right now I just wanted my sister back home with us. She didn't know any better and I wish that I could go in front of the judge and express that to him. But with all the evidence that they had against Imani, it would be a waste of time and would probably fall back on me again.

I had also reached out to Teddy earlier and expressed how I felt about it too and he agreed with my decision also. As of now, it was best that I worked on rebuilding our relationship before anything.

I got up and grabbed my car keys so that I could put the letter in my car. I wanted to drop it off at the post office first thing in the morning before my day got started. As I walked the halls of my house, I just smiled to myself. Everything was clean and the aroma in the house smelled so good and I thanked Kenya everyday about that. Also knowing that mother was upstairs sleeping peacefully in a bed made me feel good inside too. All we were missing now was Imani. She didn't have a life sentence and I knew that once her bid was up, everything was going to go back to normal again. I could feel it.

After dropping the letter on the passenger seat, I decided to walk up to the yard to check the mailbox. It had been so long since I did that and getting in the habit of doing it again definitely made everything feel like home.

I pulled out a stack of envelopes and I was for sure that 95% of them were bills again. We had so much things to get back in the habit of doing that I couldn't imagine what those letters were about. Even though Kenya stayed on top of the major bills, some of them just wouldn't stop coming in.

After going through the stack, I found one that stood out to me the most and my heart lit up. It was a letter from Imani that was written to everyone and I couldn't wait to open it. I quickly walked back in the house because I was so excited to hear from her and it was a coincidence that I wrote her already. I looked at the time and it was only 10:30pm so I decided to wake everyone up before it go too late.

Imani was still family and I wanted everyone to know that regardless of what she was in there for. However we could show her support, I wanted to do just that.

After finally rounding everyone up, I stood in the center of the living room tearing the envelope a part like a kid opening a birthday gift.

"What is it? Is everything okay?" Layla asked while rubbing her eyes.

"Yes everything is okay. It's a letter from Imani. She wrote it out to all of us so I wanted us to be here together once I read it out loud," I said with excitement in my voice.

"Baby, we could've waited until the morning for that. We all had a long day and we need to rest. Seriously?" I could hear the annoyance in Kenya's voice.

Even though I was on board with forgiving and starting over with Imani, Kenya wasn't. She was still feeling nonchalant about the situation and I couldn't fault her for that either.

Her and Imani had been tight for years and when everything had hit the fan, it hurt her bad. She never once asked about her or showed any interest in Imani after my release. And since momma been in the house with us, her and Layla had been too busy with her to even care about Imani. I didn't mind it though so I allowed her to deal with it the best way she knew how. I knew that sooner or later that she would come around so I didn't push the issue too much. Kenya was good at heart so I knew that she just needed some time.

"No we can't wait because there's no telling how long that

letter had been sitting in that damn box. Do you see this here?" I held up the stack of mail that I had in my hand.

Kenya rolled her eyes and placed one hand on her hip and exhaled deeply. I knew that she didn't care but at this point, I didn't care. They were all up and standing on their two feet so five minutes of their time wasn't going to kill them.

Momma was excited just as much as I was so she was basically all the hype man that I needed right now.

"Whatever. Well go ahead. I have things to do in the morning and Layla has school too. Don't forget that," she said.

I ignored her attitude and started reading the letter out loud.

To everyone who was affected by my cruel behavior,

First and foremost, I don't want anyone feeling any kind of pity or crying over me. This is indeed my karma and I have recently accepted that. For years, I have spent my life cheating people out of things that they valued the most in their lives. Some things that I am even ashamed of confessing that I did. My actions were followed by me always wanted to feel love. I wanted to feel important and be on top just like any successful person out there. I fucked up when I went against the ones who loved and cared about me the most to gain all of that though. Today was officially the day of self-evaluation and I spent it crying, praying, and meditating through it all. Asking God for forgiveness and also praying to the ones who lives I took away from them and ruined. If I could turn back the hands of time, I definitely would've loved myself first so that I could do the same to others. I never knew how to love myself and because of that, I created a damn disease in my heart that I couldn't get rid of. Which we all know it as: HATE! That disease caused so many people close to me so much harm and I wish that I could take the pain away from you all. But now it's too late, I know it is. So because of that I made the decision to punish myself in a way that most would say that I would deserve of course and that's fine. Again, please don't cry for me. It wouldn't be fair that I should live to enjoy the luxury of being taken care of by the state while the people I hurt the most still have to morn and struggle to recover from everything that I have destroyed in their lives. To Carter my dear brother and Kenya my best-friend, I am so sorry. Believe me, I am. You guys are the perfect example of black true love and I obviously envied that. I should've been a friend instead of an enemy because now I don't get to watch you guys inspire other couples out there and to celebrate the gifts of life with you guys also. I know that my apology won't change anything but at least when I am gone, I would be able to rest in peace knowing that I made the attempt to say it. Please continue to love, support, and manifest all of you guys dreams together regardless of anyone out there. I don't know anyone else out there who could do it better than you guys so I want y'all to keep going strong like you always have. To conclude this, I am not sure where my soul is going after this but I know that I will see you guys one day. Whether it is heaven or hell. I am okay with it because I deserve all of this and this is my punishment to myself. At least now I am able to finally let all of that hate out of my heart and destroy that disease forever. I will never infect another person again and that also brings me peace. Truly, I am sorry.

Please pray for my soul. I love you guys,
Imani AKA Marissa

THE END

CPSIA information can be obtained
at www.ICGtesting.com
Printed in the USA
LVHW041537011020
667692LV00002B/420